NEW QUOIN

Great Desires *for* Absent Things

NEW QUOIN
dba AutoNovus
PO Box 90
Cross River NY 10518

Published 2010
in the United States of America

ISBN 978-0-615-33873-6

Great Desires *for* Absent Things

A Novel

Rob Ryser

To the still suffering alcoholic…
do not fear to hope

Special Acknowledgement

To the men and women of God
who have been such wonderful ambassadors
of the second chance life.

Publisher's Note

"The enemy often supplies us
with great desires for absent things
to divert our minds from present things,
from which, small as they may be,
we might obtain great profit."

— St. Francis de Sales

Book One

ENCLOSURE

Trying to Solve an Enigma

The first thing they told us when we got here was that we were on a holy mountain. All the Franciscan brothers in the brown habits nodded in affirmation. Next I thought they were going to tell us to take off our shoes. "Recognize where you are," the brother superior told us. "If a starving man has a hundred-dollar bill in his pocket but he doesn't recognize it, he dies." I recognize where I am all right. It's the road leading me here that's the paradox. It seems like the whole purpose of putting down the drink a year ago was so that I could hit the wall all the harder today, *without* the anesthesia.

I have more problems now than I did drunk.

I don't mean to be hard on this place. I might stay indefinitely if I could. The pine forests and the wild fields with orange August flowers are like heaven to me, but I never would have come to a monastery apart from my unbelievable dilemma. Ori Alexander had to twist my arm and lobby the retreat leaders to let me in, because I'm not yet a full partner in sobriety, but even that didn't clinch it. It was my own desperation and a trick of circumstance that made me put all my hope in getting some divine answer here, which I realize now has no guarantee of appearing. The only guarantee is that at the end of this retreat, I have to go home to my wife Cicero and tell her whether I've decided to accept her impossible mission.

My cell is tiny, and everything in it is miniature. All the cells on the seventh floor are this size. The Franciscan brothers used to live here before they built the huge Maximilian Kolbe Center next door. Now these cells are plain prayer retreat rooms, except for mine, which has the air of a collision. At first I thought the commotion in here came from the texture clash of contrasting wallpaper patterns with the raised-grain maple paneling and the beaded molding and the fussy ribbed window fabric bunched on a gold rod. But as I focus on the detail, the design draws me to wonder.

This black-and-white lattice-pattern wallpaper, for example, has alternating squares that are filled with soft-edged daisies of the opposite block color, which in turn are anchored with center dots of white or black. It's too much geometry for a cell this size, but something about its placement next to this reed-themed wallpaper suggests order. The reed paper has broad gray horizon lines, random-weaved with vertical red cords and thick aqua-olive bars. The pattern looks like wind-thrown meadow grass. It's somehow integrated with the silver clamshell towel rack holders and the louver closet doors and the chain-suspended shelf over the bed. The monk in here before me brought this room to an odd conclusion.

It makes my brain ache to think of connections I didn't make soon enough: How my boy Marco retreats into secluded gloom the third week of January when we had the date set on his head for the abortion; how I used to think I was ahead of my time and smarter than the common guy when in fact I lived on a stolen watch and wanted none of the effort it takes to be self-made; how I used to believe what Charlie Gul told me, when the truth is that people who go out of their way to give you advice about your life have already avoided the same advice about their own.

Originally the retreat leaders assigned me to one of the plain white cells down the hall, but when I passed by this room, I knew I had to have it. I went back downstairs, through the time-warp vestibule from the old Friary to the Kolbe Center, and down two flights of hard steps to the orientation table, where Skip the Nametagger and Frank the Forward Gay were sitting with the same expressions as an hour before, and I told them, "Look if it's no problem let me switch to Room 27, please." When Skip began a friendly-enough response that anyone could see was going to lead to "no," Gay Frank exhaled an 'I've have it up to here' sigh, gave me the key, and said "Just don't tell anybody and hurry up," which I did without saying thanks, because whatever had crept up Gay Frank's throat didn't concern me. Except that it was meant to be.

It occurs to me that by changing rooms, Origen Alexander won't be able to find me and harass me until dinner. Even if he does, there's a monk-made SILENCE PLEASE sign outside my door, which to me means no knocking. It certainly forbids the shouting out that Origen is prone to. In truth, Ori's shouting out is forbidden in AA too. It's only because he's 10 years sober that he's tolerated. But he's really not tolerable, because of what he did to Cara Kole and what she did to him. Ori has you believe the stuff they did to each other was pathologically inevitable, because Ori is a science zealot who compiles banker's boxes full of research abstracts and journal articles and tear sheets from *Pharma Daily* in his two-room flat above The Village Tabard. But biochemistry and the human genome can't fix the bad bridge between him and the girl. Science isn't interested in the human condition because it wouldn't know it if it saw it. Yet Ori leans on his science all the more religiously, although he won't admit it. Psychology is his spirituality. Microbiology is his philosophy. Quantum theory his mystery. Ori awaits the unified theory of physics with the expectation of the second coming of Christ. Somebody should tell Ori that Christ will bring the unified theory with him when he comes.

If I practiced what I preached, I wouldn't let Ori's knock go unopened, as my wife Cicero is constantly telling me to do. Because the truth is I would have left AA if it wasn't for him. Ori got his hand up in a meeting early in my sobriety after the old AA leader Bob Frighthairs trashed me for 'comparing' instead of 'identifying' with a drunk who had just whined about not having a driver's license. At the time I knew Ori by his voice that came at you like it was under water. It had a calming effect on you, even while his pompous vocabulary would repel you. His word choice was so septic like his hero James Joyce that half of what he said died in your ears.

Ori said in my defense at that AA meeting: “When I landed here and saw this act I thought ‘Hey, I can do this.’ So I joined your bad acting club. Then after coming around for awhile I saw my own act sitting in my chair asking me what I was looking at, and I joined the *really bad* acting club.”

Then Ori got in the good dig on AA that when people need help, we coupon them. ‘Easy does it.’ ‘Keep it simple.’ ‘One day at a time.’ ‘Let go and let God.’ A coupon. Something with apparent value to redeem later. If you last that long. After the meeting, Ori told me that the secret of staying sober was not changing into somebody else, but knifing the people who did. It got my mind off me and kept me thinking enough to come back. I stayed in AA. I kept my newspaper job.

But maybe there is such a thing as too much thinking. Maybe being a newspaper reporter makes me force connections that aren’t there. It was Charlie Gul’s idea that I might be good at journalism, because of all my opinions. “You need to do something with all your opinions,” he told me, his glass of Bacardi raised to his forehead as if to extract the thought. “There’s nothing more pathetic than a bartender at three in the morning with opinions.” But a newspaper reporter doesn’t write his own opinions. He writes other people’s opinions. And journalism doesn’t care for the truth, only the facts. So in fact there is something more pathetic than a bartender with opinions at three in the morning, and that's newspaper reporter with his own ideas. Worthless ideas. Without even a bar anymore to launch them.

People forget that I was a good bartender, in spite of what I lifted. I was never the type to guess what people drank, but I could tell them *why* they drank. They thought that was genius, but it was only a matter of observation and connection. I still watch seven times before I speak. And I don't lie to anyone anymore, except about how my eye got poked blind.

I can't get over how everything in this monk cell is junior-size: the shin-high bed; the kid dresser; the kick bucket garbage can with the wheel of vertical tongue depressors around the rim. The shaving mirror is adjusted to adult height, however, and I do not technically lie about it. The thing with my eye *was* an accident. I could've prevented it. Possibly.

But I can't tell people the truth about my eye without telling my entire war story, and I'm not about to do that, because the war stories drunks tell are torture. Besides, if you look at the accident with my eye in isolation, you would say that I deserved it, and the truth is not as simple as that. It takes a hell of a lot of explaining, anyway, as Cicero my wife could tell you. I got my eye poked blind by my wife's bad half-sister Odessa Cruz seven years ago, and I'm still explaining what happened to Cicero. My life was a Thunderbird inferno, for crying out loud. But Cicero insisted she was the injured one. I'm the one with the damn prosthetic eye. At the time, I was not about to open my head and show Cicero everything inside it, because she would only use it against me. It got to the point where my wife dyed her hair fire blonde and bedded a dentist for me to realize that her suspicion about my eye wouldn't die if I starved it. On the contrary, it feasted on the silence. But that changed when I got into Alcoholics Anonymous and I figured out that the recovery program consisted of getting right with God, getting right with others, and getting straight myself. That intrigued Cicero, and she dropped her wise ass about my recovery — even though she still thought my will was weak and the AA program was a placebo. She stopped dogging me because she's an intelligent girl and she saw her restitution coming.

"How?" Cicero said when we were in bed. "How are you going to get right with others, Baby?"

"One step at a time." It was one of those nights at nine in the summer when we were waiting for dark to touch each other.

"I want to know everything while I still have a life to live."

I heard exactly what she was saying so I told her: "You have to give time time, girl. This ain't like getting your teeth fixed."

She didn't like that and left bed for her mother's house, because she felt that the dentist was my fault. But we did talk more in the next months as I took my steps in the AA program, and as Marco moved in with us full time on High Street when Odessa got deathly sick. Now Cissy is pressing hard again. I have this sense of her always over my shoulder — Cicero has only an inch of height over me, but it feels like more. She keeps asking "Are you on your ninth yet?"

The ninth step is the peak of the program where you confess your wrong to people you've hurt without making excuses. The golden boys in AA brag to the rest of us in the shadows of recovery that it is not a monumentally difficult step because it's all about cleaning up your side of the street. Well fine. Except you don't hear from the people who go to jail or the grave for a backfired ninth step confession. You only hear about the cats who go back out drinking because, God forbid, they didn't take to the program full-throttle. I've been on my eighth step for three months. That's why Ori had to raise Lazarus to get me in here. This retreat is only for AA men with all 12 steps.

It's not that I can't tell Cicero what happened, but that it's so unnecessary. I mean, the pain it would cause everyone would serve no purpose. When Odessa dies, Cicero and I will surely take custody of Marco, by mutual agreement, and that will be the end of it. And Odessa *is* dying. It took Flaco eight months to go from the couch to the grave once his T-cells dropped under 300. It's true that Flaco drank Thunderbird and smoked gutter butts until the day he left the Porticoes on York and came to die here at the Inn on this holy mountain, and that Odessa, with her organic brown rice tea and vegan shakes, watches everything that goes into her body. But health doesn't matter with AIDS.

On Christmas Eve Odessa's T-cells were 145. The girl is 23 and her life is over.

I'll tell you what Odessa did. It was a rib. A lamb rib. With the meat still on it. It was a rack of lamb off a plate at the restaurant and she grabbed it by the meat end and swung it back at me, bone first, like an ice pick. The blood squirted through her fingers. It wasn't my blood. It was the blood from the lamb. Her first jab hit my sclera, which was luck, because she couldn't see where she was swinging, and her second roundhouse was way off and hit me in the temple before I figured out she had something in her hand, and I smashed her wrist hard on the tiles until she broke down crying and finally dropped it. Then I let her go. I told her to get the hell away.

See, everyone tells me I should have gone right away to Beth Israel and showed them what happened, but what everybody forgets is that it was my 21st birthday that night, and I had lifted $660 from the bar and I wasn't about to waste it on some emergency room crooks when the whole point was Odessa was really grabbing for the steak knife and could've killed me with her wild swinging. I was a stupid alcoholic, but I wasn't dumb. I told people I was jumped. Which was not all a lie. I was not going to tell Cicero that I was plowing her half sister on the terrace at Quo Vadis when suddenly Odessa went mad like her butcher father, Brutus Cruz, and tried to kill me. As long as I didn't go to Cicero, Odessa wouldn't tell her scary old man.

It wasn't until Monday morning after my birthday that I woke up and couldn't see out of my right eye. But that night, Saturday night, like I said, it was my birthday and I had $660 that I lifted from the bar and more of the same Thai stick that made Odessa flip but that I was sailing on, except for minor throbbing and these yellow-purple rings around my right orbit, which I thought had as much to do with the pot and the bloody dent in my temple as it did with the gouge in the white of my eye. So I bought a bottle of Thunderbird on First Avenue and forgot about going to the West Side to meet Cicero, because I knew she would kill the night when she saw my eye. I went to the Porticoes on York, where I knew I would at least find Flaco, who had the wasting disease bad by then and didn't move off the couch unless it rained.

The Porticoes is what we called the old lot on York at 68th Street where a builder left the facade of a porch with five arches and columns near a dump of old desks, filing cabinets and swivel chairs. When I got to the Porticoes on York that night it was just the colonnade and me. I didn't want to be alone in my high-backed swivel chair under the faint stars with another hot Sunday arriving and no one to tell me what I needed to hear: '*Your eye's fine*,' or '*Odessa won't tell*,' or '*Six-sixty lift is nothing—I know guys who lift twelve hundred a night*.' That night I was so lonely I would have welcomed the sight of Cicero through the Porticoes. Instead, it was Charlie Gul, the scumbag poet, who was the last person I should have wanted to see that night, but I didn't suspect him then.

Outside my cell is a courtyard with a partition of young elm trees on the ridge, and rock outcroppings the size of baby elephants on one side of a narrow path that cuts slightly uphill to the summit chapel. Then up to my right, as I bend my neck under the raised window sash, I see it: a rising bell tower with a gray stucco facing and slender stone column accents spaced between high hollow window arches, leading to a Spanish tile roof and a white cross at the top. It is a luring sight, though I am under strain in this position, and I get on my knees to improve my angle. In just this moment, I feel the peace again that came to me the night I stayed up listening to Origen explain how AA is counterintuitive – how you have to surrender to win and become powerless to overcome. Just like the Gospel. It's the peace that chills the back of your neck, as if you're being tickled with frost; it comes with the sensation of warmth and fullness that you feel being at home at last after a long time away.

But now it departs from me, without showing its trail.

This is what I dread.

And yet this is what I've come to expect. I find peace by looking at the old bell tower and it evaporates as soon as I try to capture it. That is why I'm such a fool to think that a weekend in a mountain top monastery five miles from Peekskill is going to deliver me from this fix. I presume too much. I expect more than my share. Maybe Ori is right: there is no praying to God for his will because God has already given me everything I'm going to get. The voices of sobriety that have enclosed my brain for the last year sing 'One day at time, brother.' But it doesn't apply. Here I am, squarely in my cell, focused in the now. I make my petition, but the answer behaves like the wind – higher than I am. Staying in the present where God speaks is too difficult for someone like me.

I see a backyard on High Street with a grove of second-growth stick trees that the attack vines have yanked down to helpless leaf shags. I see the knee-high buttercups on thin stems at the break of the woods. I remember the burst of wild mint that takes me by surprise each time I mow it over. And I hear the shrieks of Marco in the kitchen, screaming as he is, because I cut down all the buttercups. He wanted to gather them up and dance and sing 'La-La-La' the way Cinderella does on the video. Of course the flowers I pick up off the lawn and give to him are no good, even though they're fine.

"He wanted to pick the buttercups," Odessa berates me in her low voice over Marco's howls. "He's only three."

"He wants to do what Cinderella does." I felt there was something disordered about a boy who wore out a Cinderella video watching it repeatedly. I mean, the kid not only knew Cinderella's lines but wanted the wand and the ball gown and the glass slippers for his birthday.

"Do you want him to grow up unfeeling like you?" Odessa said. "That's so sexist that a boy can't like Cinderella."

"Is that how you got in at Quo Vadis?"

"Are you joking?"

"The only girl to get a job on the floor in 10 years, and you got the job that day."

"You bring that up now?"

"You weren't exactly Miss Androgynous when you interviewed."

"That was a long time ago."

"That was four years ago."

"You cut down my boy's flowers — "

"In my yard — "

"You apologize to him or I'm not bringing him over anymore."

My instinct was to wait for Cicero to say something, but Cicero obviously wasn't there. Cicero loathes Odessa. Even more today, now that Odessa is so religious.

"Come here," I had said to Marco, who quieted down when he heard Odessa tell me to apologize. "Come on."

I took him to the front yard and down the hill to the Depot Square to buy something better than buttercups, but when I stopped at the hardware store and showed him the rainbow bubble lawnmower, he got all rigid and obstinate again until I grabbed hold of the little toy and said "When you put the bubbles in here and you start to push – see?" Marco liked that. I knew he would. "And we'll get one of these, too." I took a skinny banana-yellow fungo bat and whiffle ball from a barrel. "When we're done mowing, we can play baseball." He howled "Noooooo!" and dropped to the sidewalk with his knees pumping, so I popped the whiffle ball out of the plastic and ripped a line drive into the street that made a cracking sound in our ears.

"Now," I said. "Let's get the ball and you do that."

When he took my hand, I had it for good that afternoon. He'd take me over the buttercups, and he'd take me over Cinderella. I knew the problem was his father's problem, not being an influence in his life, but I could never tell that to Odessa. She would only turn it around and say to me, "Well, why don't *you* do something, Bub?"

From the start, I have been the closest thing Marco has had to a dad, and it is not nearly enough. I know Marco is mine, but it's never been my advantage to claim him. Cicero would leave me for sure, and Brutus Cruz would kill me. At least he's always said he would kill whoever did it, but what he would really do is make sure I never saw Marco. That was not a big threat when drinking was a friend and a titan, but it is now. Marco has been living with us since Thanksgiving, and there's a tenderness about him, in spite of his broken home, which is an uplifting thing.

He's been an inspiration for Cicero, too, and changed her thinking about us. Before Marco moved in, it was enough for Cicero to go to work with the kids at school and talk about how we would do everything differently as parents. But after Thanksgiving I noticed adjustments in Cicero's vocabulary, calling the pill 'stupid' once, and whispering 'I want you to come inside me' the night we celebrated my third month sober. Then there was the one night I got back after one in the morning from an AA meeting and Cicero was still awake in bed. She wasn't angry about me being two hours late without calling, which made me nervous. Cicero stays calm right up to her explosions, so you can't tell that she's building up — a strategy she borrowed from her real father who died in a boat fire. So I was ready. She said in an upbeat tone, over the wet rattle of our air-conditioner: "Sometimes late can be good."

I thought it was her sarcasm so I kept quiet and stayed on my edge of the bed. She said it again, the same words, so I apologized to her: "I was talking to Ori."

“I said being late can be good.”

I should have figured out that she was telling me something. But my head on the pillow went swimming in Ori’s sea of trouble, and then Cicero did get angry. About everything. And it wasn’t until the morning that I saw the pregnancy test box in the bathroom garbage and understood what she told me three times.

“Can’t you say something besides ‘That’s great’?” She said.

“Yeah,” I told her. The first thing I thought was: ‘Does this mean you don’t want your Ph.D.?’ But I didn’t have the courage. So I said: “It’s time.”

Cicero doesn’t want to shock Marco’s insecurities with the new baby. She wants to adopt Marco now and make a big deal of it before her belly shows. If Cicero is anything, she’s a psychologist. She’s got it all worked out how she’s going to tell Marco in stages. I trust she’s right, because her mother, Emily Cruz, concurs. And if Emily Cruz is anything, she is her daughter’s dearest friend.

The problem is that Cicero wants me to go get Odessa’s permission to adopt Marco. Everyone starting with Odessa and ending with her butcher father Brutus Cruz wants it to be that way eventually. No one except Cicero has so crassly asked for it to be brought out now.

If Cicero would just mind her own business and not mess with the inevitable, Odessa would die and we would be sad for Marco, but we would make it up to him on High Street, and the violent way he was conceived could no longer hurt people.

Things occur to me in retrospect that I should have said to avoid this trap, but I can’t be diverted with them now. Cicero has worn me down to my very word. It chills me to think about a meeting with Odessa, because all I can see is her venom and Marco's shock and Cicero's rage and the butcher's threats and my own retreat down to Washington Square Park in the Village where that sick dick Charlie Gul will find me first, and I'll forget who I am and why I care.

My ears ring with the last words Cicero whispered today before I left High Street: 'Before I show.'

"Refuge for the guilty."

It's the subsurface voice Ori Alexander in the courtyard two floors under my window. He's bent like a snake, blowing the smoke of his crap cigar above him in a dirty shroud.

"First I said to myself, 'Gee, Byline ran away.' But then I said, 'No, he's already running. He must be hiding.'"

"I didn't like my room," I tell him.

"Yeah, well, to these brothers creature comforts are the devil."

"That's not what I meant."

"Shell games, Byline. You show the pea and mix up the shells. What do I see? No pea. Wrong shell. You know why? One of us is not sincere."

"You found me, didn't you?"

"That I did, Byline. That I did."

Three Kinds of Time

When I pull my head in from the window, my cell is not the same. The light seems wrong, and I notice the orange bulletin with last Sunday's scripture readings and a quotation from Augustine about how the past and the future exist nowhere but in the mind. The bulletin must have been sitting here on the dresser when I walked in. It makes me wonder what else I've missed. I see that the Listerine with the 26.9 percent alcohol is still in the medicine cabinet.

Real smart to leave that behind for a drunk.

I wonder how long it takes to stop always thinking about drinking. In truth, thinking isn't my problem; it's lack of thinking. Here I am on a prayer retreat, looking for an answer in the room of collision, and I'm being called away by Origen to my dinner obligation.

I grip my prosthesis between my thumb and forefinger and rotate it until it clears the socket and comes out. I use the point of my pick to scrape the residue off the edge. The buildup used to accumulate until my eye got red before I cleaned it. Now I'm a little obsessive about taking care of it, because Cicero makes me that way. She reminds me how long it took to get the match right. But if you ask me, all the business about computerized coloring and custom shaping the fake eye was just a game to jack up the price on a crap plastic cap that's no better than a black patch, which is what I wanted, but Cicero refused to let me wear. When my prosthesis was ready, Cicero and Emily Cruz and the frauds at Quo Vadis acted as though it was a glass masterpiece hand-blown in Venice. It wasn't. It was painted blood vessels on acrylic. 'Oh, it looks too real, Bobby,' they said. No one tells you the truth in those situations. I told them all to shut up.

This business about your other senses kicking in to compensate when you lose your sight is a lot of dog eggs, too, because the truth is that when you lose your sight, all you can see is the past and the future. AA calls it a victory if you can defeat the forces of memory and expectation and face the present. But that doesn't work for me, in spite of my effort. So Augustine can be right that there is no past or future, and the AA promise can stand that if you work the program right, you won't regret your past or wish to shut the door on it. For me, it's more wind to chase. I *am* still angry that Odessa Cruz blinded my eye, and that Marco's hurt is out of my reach, and that I can't have the bar I dream about or the girl who wanted it for me. I'm trapped by Ori who's going to dive off the Golden Gate Bridge if I abandon him. By a meddling mother-in-law and her second husband muscle who wants to wrestle me. By Phyllis Stein my editor at the damn newspaper who's scarier when she wants to hug you than when she wants to hang you. By Charlie Gul, the two-timing poet who never wrote an honest verse in his life — not even in the beginning, when I so foolishly followed him.

Who did I forget? Oh yes: Cicero, who has still not taken back what she said the day she cut her hair, about me being just like my father.

My father, Adamo Dante, is a man of great starts. Great starts. But I wouldn't be here at Goloborza if I was like my father. And I sure wouldn't be psyched about having a baby with Cicero or wanting Marco to live with us if all I cared about was my own designs. Besides, who would call my last year in AA a great start? The dregs who came into the program at the same time I did a year ago have their 12 steps and are sponsoring newcomers already. I swear, for all of Cicero's instinct, her insight sucks. I intend to finish what I started, in spite of what Ori Alexander says. That's the difference between him and me.

I put my eye back in and lock my cell door behind me. Down the hallway past the SILENCE PLEASE sign is a four-foot wooden cross on the wall and a painted corpus of Christ looking skyward with great strain on his brow. Down six steps to a landing is a smaller statue of St. Francis in ecstasy, his arms crossed at the wrists so that his hands with their bloody marks make a butterfly pattern over his chest. He, too, is looking up, but in awe. I wish I didn't have the steel heels on my boots, because the racket they make on these steps echoes down the stairwell, signaling to anyone with ears my loud descent, even though as I cross the threshold, I have left the Enclosure of the Friary, and am no longer bound to silence.

There is no one down the arched yellow hallway of offices with frosted glass windows that leads to the time-warp vestibule, and the low-hanging dome lamps give a surreal light that tugs at me as if I am being called out of the present.

You have to go through two doors, climb three steps and go down three steps in the vestibule to cross a space of only a few feet, and when you are in between doors and see the windows with their metal trim painted London-red, you can easily imagine yourself in an English phone box or a double-decker bus or at least somewhere over there where she went and you said you would follow, but you didn't. I don't know why I think of my mother at the times I do. I don't think awful much of my mother. She was going to Leeds whether I followed or not.

The dining hall is ahead of me, down the high wide passageway that opens to the West with six-foot windows. Through them, a twilight haze over the Hudson River mutes the pink setting sky.

I see Origen before he notices me. He's leaning on the wall in wire-rim glasses with black lenses that pick up the white reflection of the hall lights. The worn gray MIT sweatshirt is from his dad's school, and Ori's forehead is a furrowed, massive thing. His rat ears sit low on his jowls, and his throat is red where his beard has always fought him.

Ori is one of these guys who will recite with great delight the highest purposes of science and yet bend over to foul detail about how Cara Kole had him sodomize her before everything between them went south, or about how masturbating is worse than the unspeakable loneliness of his nights alone above The Village Tabard, because no one touches Ori except Ori. And even that has become a grotesque chore. A horrifying obligation. It's not a playful indulgence or a healthy diversion or a therapeutic escape. It's a monstrosity. When it's over, Ori's loathing is worse than Ammon's, because there is no Tamar to throw out, and Ori's only lift from the pit of self disgust is the certainty that he has no choice: a man who nobody touches needs to be touched, even though touching himself makes him all the more untouchable.

It's something I don't debate him about because it falls under a taboo category called Things I know more about than Ori: it takes all the skill a man has to excite a mind that is bloated with pornography.

For the man, arousal must engage the *will.* Nowhere but in that deep faculty is there enough capacity to feed an addiction of diminishing return. Nothing short of the absolute illicit will bring satisfaction: it's lawlessness that stimulates arousal. The girl in the man's head must be someone else's. She must be *taken.* Must she be a knockout? No, that's not the point.

Our bodies are wired in unsearchable ways; everything we do with them touches God.

Ori has a *Nature* magazine face-high between him and the dining hall. God forbid some incremental advance in string theory should get past his attention on retreat and take him out of the loop. Nobody reads *Nature* for fun but Ori. He says he has his files to keep. Files for his book. But his files aren't for that. He needs to cover himself when he dies. He tells me "When I die they'll say 'Yeah, this guy didn't count for zero, but at least he was on the right track.'" Ori imagines I'm some secretary who will confirm him in the end. Somewhere in his crap flat there's a file on me. And somewhere in that file, I'm supposed to say what is already scripted.

"Byline, you ducked out of our scene without saying your line."

I don't know what line he's talking about, but it isn't worth chasing on the weak chance that he means something clever instead of cruel. We both stand at the cafeteria doors, intimidated by the size of the crowd.

"There must be something else going on," I say it to myself as much as to him. There are hundreds in the hall — almost all men. "Can all this be Matt Talbot?"

It's the size of a gymnasium in here, with a glass wall of west-facing windows that draws the hills of the Hudson Highlands into the room, and thick arching columns painted bright plum that support the vaulted ceiling. An icon of the Last Supper with figures in gold, indigo and scarlet spans the southern wall, and I feel the noise of five voices on top of me, but I look around and can't trace where a single one comes from. Ori and I ladle chicken rice soup into our bowls and take handfuls of crackers off the side table, because the buffet is backed up. We unstack two chrome-frame chairs with lemon seats from the plastic 1970s and sit near the podium, with the bowls on our laps.

"This beats the can," Ori says. He thinks the kitchen made the soup from stock.

"I need more than this," I tell him. "I'm starving."

"Well, you know what *he* said about that."

"Who?"

"Who do you think?"

I look up at the icon of Christ and again am made to feel like the dope who doesn't get it quick enough, so I snap, "He said a lot, didn't he?"

"He said *you* feed them." Ori's jaw is clenched.

This is where Ori and I don't agree — this revisionist liquid he applies to revelation and miracles. This is why Ori won't pray. Won't trust the church or admit the evidence around him that God can change lives in the midst of failings and would do it in Ori's own life if he would ask.

Ori thinks the multiplication of the loaves is allegory.

"Then he did a miracle." I tell him.

"Good, Byline. The miracle was that people *shared* what they had."

"And when they had nothing to share in the desert, God dropped bread from heaven."

"Yes and no, Byline. The people wanted meat, so God gave them quail until it came out of their nostrils. They died with the bird between their teeth. Don't ask for what you've already been given."

There's a stirring to my left at the podium where two of the brothers are engaged with a woman wearing a tasseled leather vest who apparently represents these other people who I couldn't peg when we walked in, because they look like they belong in an L.L. Bean catalogue.

These men at the tables who are with us for the Matt Talbot retreat don't dress in the worn clothes of old drinkers anymore like the men do with the bad backs who run the buffet gear for the kitchen. The runners still have the skin sores and downward stares of habbers 10 days sober, and they're here doing food service for their program at the Inn down the mountain. Each runner has crossing thoughts in his head like '*don't drop the potatoes,*' and '*ask Brother if he's finished first and* THEN *take the plate.*' Inevitably runners get overwhelmed and stop in midcourse. I understand that. I understand these rehab runners. I don't know who these hippies are but they don't belong here. This is a fact-finding, truth-facing mission, not some self-propelled exercise in proper spiritual posture.

"Let's go," I tell Ori, getting up from my seat. "Come on."

"Not now, Byline. The prayer."

I'm already walking to the buffet and I may as well keep moving away from Origen, because he's right: a tall brother with bifocals and a silver wreath of hair reaches the podium an arm's length from where I would have been seated with soup on my lap and 300 people watching.

At the buffet, a thick whiskered Inn Man running the squash is on overload. He has nowhere to set down the new tray, and he can't take up the old one. This is how we get sober. First we figure out the squash. I'll bet he doesn't even like squash, yet his whole life has come down to this dish that's behaving like Goliath. Try telling him there's no past or future. If there is only one kind of time, he isn't fit for it, because what he wants to do is spike the tray and high step down the hill past his fellow Inn Men for the next train back to the Bowery.

He has been saved by the dings of forks on glass, as the hall quiets for the tall silver brother. Ori reads *Nature* while guiding his souped-up spoon into his mouth. His hair bristles are erect at attention. I don't know how many times he's told me he would never trust anything in the hands of the Catholic Church.

The silver brother announces the hippies as members of the Hudson Valley Shakespeare Festival. *Actors*! Next, a California group of Buddhists. Then Presbyterians for an ecumenical conference. He welcomes us last as the Matt Talbot 24s. The silver brother prays, thanking the Provider for his provision, and the hall volume climbs back to the surround-sound pitch that has me looking again for the source of the voices on top of me.

"*Buddhists*," I tell Ori when he comes up to the buffet.

"Yeah, Byline, so?"

The runner is still hunched in his tracks on my blind side, so I extend my plate to him with one hand saying, 'Here,' and I support his pan with the palm of my other hand which stings like all hell and then shoots a burning rope up my arm that I bear inside. It takes the runner a second more to grab my plate, so that I get my free fingers on the handles. We stand here a moment. I feel the moistness on my forehead from the shock of the burn.

"Men?" Ori takes my plate from the runner. Now the runner sees the solution. He takes up the empty tray, nods to Ori, and doesn't wait to confirm that I complete the little chore as he retreats to the kitchen.

"Byline, you can't pull the wagon if you're still in the wagon."

"Now you sound like Jared."

"Revolting as that is, Byline, the fact is that God works through whoever he wants and that includes Buddhists, and Jared of the Sorrows and these clowns from the Bard club. You burned yourself, didn't you."

Jared of the Sorrows is my incredibly unpopular sponsor who told me to get the pornography out of my head the night I asked him to take me through the 12 steps. He thinks less of Ori than Ori thinks of him, which is a hell of a thing to say when you consider that the boys in the Friday nightclub call Jared "S.K." for Storm King, because a cloud follows him everywhere he goes.

The Friday night boys aren't bright. I mean, none of them except maybe Pete the Breeze and me are going to make it. The cloud is God's cloud, and it brings rain on the saved and the cursed. There is no getting away from it, and there is no way I can go back to the old way of doing things.

It's like Jared taught me — you can't drink on the truth and you can't stay sober on a lie.

He's right. What am I going to do, go back to that pretender Charlie Gul and his Avenue A fraud? He would grin at me with those unclean teeth and say 'Can the deceived be happy?' The question always seemed bigger than me, because I assumed the answer was 'yes.' I never figured he was talking about himself, or that the answer might be 'no' — hell no.

The deceived can never be happy.

Just as we sit, a crash of plates in the kitchen makes Ori and me jump. The things must have been stacked too high. It's an amateur kitchen — I could tell when I walked in.

My father was going to teach me how to run a four-season restaurant the summer I turned 19 when he opened The State on Rush Street in Chicago. The one time I remember being alone with him that whole summer was a week before the opening. We were both in kitchen whites, drinking Remy from ramekins for some reason in a walk-in refrigerator the size of my little Friar's cell. We talked about the change of the seasons.

I've always wanted to be in the kitchen and understand my father's genius, but I wound up behind the bar suffering his weakness.

"Yeah, well, Byline. Fatherhood. That's the real issue, isn't it?"

My lips must be moving. "Whose?"

"Yours. What are you laughing at?"

"Nothing. In seven months maybe." It occurs to me that I haven't updated the math in my head. Cicero is due on Valentine's Day, which is six months away. "Or sooner."

"I mean now, Byline."

"What are you talking about?"

"This fantasy to rescue the maiden from the dragon."

I made the mistake of telling Origen that Cicero wants me to ask Odessa for permission to adopt Marco, and that I was thinking about doing a ninth step confession with Odessa.

"Great desires for absent things," Ori's shaking his head at me. "You'd rather be the myth than the man."

"Why, because I do the tough confessions?"

Forget Hippocrates and doing no harm – they threw out his bag in the seventies. What does the program say?"

Everybody knows what the program says. It forbids a ninth step confession when it could harm someone. That always means ex-girlfriends. And he's right. The old girlfriend prohibition is a legitimate excuse for me to avoid Odessa, even though I'm not worried about rekindling any attraction.

"This is something *Cicero* wants," I tell him.

In the upturned snarl of his eyebrows I see the distrust he's always had for me. Let him suspect I'm Marco's father all he wants. He knows no more about it than Cicero. He only thinks he does.

"This is something *you* want," Ori says. "You need to know that you could still have the little tart."

Disturbing Questions

I had to leave Ori in the hall, because even though he apologized when I shot up to leave, he immediately scolded me for punishing him by walking out. He attacks me as though I should be grateful that he points out my self-deceit.

But there's no truth to the Odessa crack, and there's no explaining that to Ori. The fact is that Odessa weighs 90 pounds, and her toes get so numb that if she trips in the infirmary she doesn't feel anything until she is falling. She has to take breath breaks between bites of food so she won't overtax herself. If she's not nauseous, she's dehydrated on account of the diarrhea, or she's fighting this reoccurring pneumonia that normally can't get past the immune system of a five-year-old.

The devil of AIDS is not the virus, it's the *opportunistic* infections.

Odessa isn't a scoop-neck blouse girl anymore, but even if she was, I'm not so desperate that I would go to her out of some need to prove my manhood when I've finally got Cicero on my side. It's preposterous. Ori's problem is that he still thinks of Odessa the way she was, and Odessa hasn't been that way since the accident on the Henry Hudson Parkway.

It doesn't register with Ori that Odessa lives in a convent, or that she can sew Deuteronomy on a pillow case, because he never knew her before the accident, even though I've told him enough war stories from Quo Vadis that he has a picture in his mind of a girl with one-in-one-hundred looks in a city of girls with one-in-one hundred looks. After Odessa and I rolled her father's Jeep on the Henry Hudson, it wasn't so much that she came out of it with scars on her face, which everybody made such a big deal over, or even that she decided to keep Marco when no one including me supported it, but that she had the same white light experience in the hospital that Bill Wilson did in 1934 before he started Alcoholics Anonymous.

No one gets that.

She is not the same girl in any way, and yet she is still 100 percent Odessa.

That's the danger. In spite of everything that has happened to her, I can't go to her safely. This is the same girl who stuck a sewing needle into my scrotum and could turn on me without warning and tell her father.

The girl who has always resented me for not leaving Cicero.

And that one night when Odessa happened to be sleeping with Cicero — I didn't have a ménage-a-trois in mind when I climbed in between them. Yes, I was drunk, but it didn't have anything to do with being drunk. I was always drunk. No one gets that either. I remember my thinking that night, because the newly wed Emily and Brutus Cruz were knocked out on whiskey and were snoring so loudly from their bedroom in the house at West Point that I couldn't stand it on the couch. I couldn't stand the thought of his hairy man chest on top of Emily, or their open mouths of cold drool, or their cute story at dinner that they met while he was watering his lawn, wearing only his black Army shorts, and she saw him barefoot in the grass and stopped her car to ask directions to Eisenhower Hall.

Made me sick.

So did their new sign on the front door: 'The Major and Mrs. Cruz.'

In the dark between my wife and Odessa, I can't say how soon I went right to sleep. But when I woke to a deep itch in my scrotum and felt the needle stuck in the skin between my testicles, I knew that Odessa had stuck me there. And Odessa knew that I knew it was her, and not merely a mistake that a needle was left behind during the quilt making, as Cicero kept insisting. It turned out to be the last time Cicero gave Odessa the benefit of the doubt.

I thought the courtyard steps that lead me out of the Maximilian Kolbe Center would be a shortcut to the Old St. Francis chapel, where a prayer service started after dinner. Instead the steps lead me the wrong way downhill to a loading dock with bats flying blind in the canyon. There is a monk at the top of the steps who's looking at me;

he knows I'm lost. He must have been watching when I took the steps down to the dock. His loose habit gives him a large stature. He knows who I am, too. I mean, he knows I'm not an actor or a Buddhist or a Presbyterian.

"I thought this was a shortcut, but I guess I have to go back the way I came." I don't like this brother. He has a school teacher's suspicion. Why can't he nod to show he understands, or smile like anyone would in greeting a guest with a little courtesy? I think he suspects me. "I'm late for prayer."

"You'll get nowhere that way." He says it like I didn't just acknowledge my own mistake.

"It's easy to get lost here." Now I know what strikes me about him. He must be twenty years younger than any Goloborza brother I've seen on this mountain. "Do *you* know your way around?"

That came out wrong, but I couldn't stop it. He makes me nervous. I bet I know why he's looking at me. It's my eye. "It's fake," I tell him, putting my forefinger on the shell without blinking. "But it's okay."

"This is our home, but we have missions all over the world," he says.

I'm stunned. So much for me telling him something personal. "It's for alcoholics," I explain.

He looks at me as though I'm lying to him. Who is this guy, the Friar police? "The chapel service I mean."

"I know."

I'm sure he does know. So why the commandeering attitude?

“To learn how to pray.” I see a switch of understanding in his eyes and figure he believes me.

“Well, I hope we can help you with that. Don’t let me stand in your way.” He nods but doesn’t move.

The school teacher brother is holding the first knot of a white rope that belts his robe and hangs down to his ankles. We’ll stand like this forever. He wants a confession.

“I shouldn’t have looked for a short cut, but, have you ever had a dilemma and feel like, you know. I don’t know.”

It’s that time of night where the light from the sky that has been phasing away in bits now fades before your eyes.

“I’m sure, brother, that you’ve had a dilemma where...well, you probably haven’t. Forget that. Have you ever prayed for a word and God was just...silent?”

“No.”

“No?” I don’t believe him.

“Do you see that ridge just over there?” He says.

“Where? No.” It’s all blackness out there.

“Closer in.”

“Oh yeah.” I don’t see anything.

“What do you see?”

God, I hate when people do this. I never get the answer right. If I’m ever in an expert position, I’ll never hold it over someone’s head like this.

“Where, brother?”

“Against the horizon, can you see?”

“Barely.”

“Trees.”

"Yeah, trees, brother."

"All the same height. What's the matter?"

"Except for that one."

"And what about it?"

"It's taller than the rest."

"What else?"

"To be honest with you I really don't –"

"Don't give up."

"Do you know, brother?"

"Do I know what?"

"Do you yourself know — wait. On the tall one — the branches are moving."

"What does that tell you?"

"That there's wind up there."

"Do you see?"

"Yeah. The high wind doesn't bother with the little trees."

"We wouldn't know about the high wind without the giants. It's the same with the spirit. We see God move in the saints. Keep your eye on the saints and God will not seem so silent. What is it?"

"Nothing."

I'm not sure what is choking me up. My mother has been trying to get me to read Butler's *Lives of the Saints* since she left. But that is not it. Something about the way I caught Marco watching me earlier today at the stove stirs up the melancholy inside.

"I'm going to be a father."

The school teacher brother brings his hand to his mouth as if for caution. The gaping sleeve falls down the bone of his wrist. Here comes another lesson.

"Do you know how to give God a good laugh?" The brother smiles. "Tell him your plans for tomorrow."

I don't know why I keep talking to this brother. His brow is creased with accusation. Then he says "Do you mean a better father?"

"I mean my wife is pregnant."

"I see now."

He only thinks he sees, and I step sideways into the grass and get past him with more ease than I anticipated, in what is now the first black of the night.

I don't owe him any parting words because he hasn't earned them, and I'm not about to turn my head around and let him think I'm some target of delusion who needs to be brought down with correction. I've already been brought down by this disease. That's why I'm here. What drunk comes on retreat to learn how to pray who isn't desperate as hell for relief and direction, for crying out loud? And what monk would oppose it though some facade of spiritual investigation?

He wasn't probing my soul, he was doubting my motive without knowing a thing about me, which is worse than what Ori does and easier than what Ori does because it doesn't require the brother to make any *connections.*

Yeah, fine. I do wish things were different between Marco and me. Even that we were closer. But I can't look into that little guy's brown eyes and tell him, '*Look kid when you were conceived your Mommy and I didn't want to keep you and you would have been aborted had it not been for the accident that scarred her face and kept her in the hospital where she had a visit from God that changed everything. And I know that you want a Daddy but I'm not married to your Mommy, and I can't act like your real Daddy because I don't know you, and you don't know me. God knows you don't know me. I know you're a good kid and the nuns think you are going to be a saint but I can only be who I am and it isn't enough.'*

I can't move on with Marco until I clear my guilt with him and I can't do that, because if I told him everything, Cicero would find out and never forgive me. Her thinking hasn't changed. Cicero would leave, and there would be no one in my life who understands what a monster this booze is to wrestle, and how it fights dirty and whispers lies in good works. Without Cissy, Jared of the Sorrows and Origen Alexander wouldn't count, because when the big things aren't in place, the little things don't matter.

Cicero went along with my dream to have my own bar, which I was going to name Julius Caesar's, but she didn't want to put off her Ph.D. at Fordham to help me get started in those first years before our problems hit. Yet Cicero was with me in a way then that I didn't appreciate until it was gone. From the beginning, she was right about me. I *wasn't* that guy with the $500-a-night in pocket and Charlie Gul's ear in the throbbing three o'clock circle at Quo Vadis — in spite of what I put Cicero through.

When Cissy fell from the fire escape and smashed her collarbone on the crossbar of a mountain bike and had to lie still in the hospital for four weeks, she lived for my little dishes.

It started out simple with vichyssoise and gazpacho to restore her core. Then something happened — her enthusiasm or mine — so that by the end of her stay I was talking a half day to make cornmeal crust sea bass or shrimp jambalaya linguini.

That was the longest time that I had been away from Cicero's bed since we met, and on the second-to-the-last night when the nurse let me stay in the room, Cicero told me in the sheets, "Baby you can *cook*." The fact that I couldn't put two legs of weight on her made the contact all the more enveloping, but it was the weeks of courtship on the plate that gave the intercourse fire like we didn't have again until I got sober.

In the furnishings of my mind, that night goes up on the fireplace mantle, so that the thought of it can still come on hard regardless of what's happening in real time. When a girl gives herself to you like that, there is nothing she withholds. It was naive of me to think that we would repeat that night in the hospital with regularity, but it was a shock to watch how far down the ladder the sex dropped in the next five years, so that I never expected Cicero's bed to inspire me again.

But lately Cissy's been on this kick where she hasn't said 'no' to me. It's more than her being off the pill. She's inspired about the pregnancy and confident that I'm doing the right thing. I haven't asked her why the shoe fits all of a sudden, because it's stupid to question a girl's confidence in you, and because Cicero doesn't volunteer stuff like that anymore. The girl likes being settled with me. And I am simply not going to yank up these roots and whisk the whole deal out to the Confession West where some promised land of rebirth awaits the brave with rewards that equal the risks.

At the edge of the grass, ten feet from the dark arched wooded door of the old St. Francis Chapel, the Talbott 24s are engaged inside, and I think I am finally onto something: I have to go back nine years to Sharon, Ohio, to remember the last time I was held this high in Cicero's esteem. It occurs to me, much as I hate it, that Origen may be right about Hippocrates and the Program: I haven't come this far to do new harm. There are twelve good ways to tell Cicero without lying that this Odessa mission is morally mean. A real slaughter of family manners. But Cicero won't agree. I can see her silver-coin earrings flash 'no' at me, insisting that I ask Odessa for Marco.

I could call Cicero's bluff and tell her if she wants me to run things on self will without prayer like before, then I don't need AA, and I can drop this sober charade, and get back to my drinking tour.

If Cissy plays hard and argues that this situation has its own ethics, I could always tell her as a last resort: 'Look, girl, I tried to get a meeting, but I'm telling you, Odessa would not have it.'

I can't let it divert me that a white lie like that is exactly the kind of situation ethics butt-liquid I used when I drank to rationalize my scams, because there is a big difference between the lie meant to deceive and the lie meant to protect. The first lie comes through the teeth. The second lie begs the hearer for mercy, because there is something more important at stake than the facts. Cicero would have to believe me or ask Odessa herself, which Cissy will never do again.

I walk into the dark chapel unprepared for the surreal arrangement of lounging bodies.

I close the low arched door and move into the slices of open floor left by spread legs and curved torsos.

The bodies face the little bald friar up at the altar, where a half dozen men recline on the floor with him. It's too dark back here to make out quickly where to go next, and I'm surrounded by the acid foot odor and scents of unwashed crotches that have sprung loose in these relaxed positions.

Most of all I small cigar breath. It isn't warm on the ear but cold, so that I cringe, knowing Origen's behind me.

"You forgot your pillow, Byline."

Another surreal sensation. Except in this case, as I examine these bodies on the floor, I see that Origen is not being scary but serious.

I *did* forget my pillow.

I don't know how all these cats knew to bring pillows. I must have missed that little instruction on my orientation sheet.

"I'll tell you what happened later," I whisper to Ori as I move up closer to the bald friar.

I have no intention of telling Origen anything, but I need to make it sound good because I don't want him to follow me, and I give him the forefinger up in the air.

He puts his forefinger up in the air, brings it to his mouth to wet it, and makes like he's turning the page in a book.

That's pantomime for Ori's theory that fools who live unexamined lives treat traumas like turning pages in a book until one day they say "Gee, this page won't turn."

It sounds like it means something, but it doesn't.

I move near the choristers where I can hear.

This is legendary Little Friar Leo, the AA darling and spiritual giant who was once a drunk like all of us.

"I'm not going to say any more tonight because I want to leave time to turn out the lights and talk to God in our own vocabularies, with our own personalities, from our own space. You see?"

His voice sounds purified, as though it has run through rocks down the mountain. "I'll just end by telling you two things that have helped me struggle with problems in my life, and they both come from the apostle Paul, who had a lot of struggles that he had to overcome in jail. Controversy in his own church. You see? And Paul put it very simply 'All things work together for good for those who love God.'"

It must be great when that coupon works. But I don't buy it.

I'm angry that I missed Little Friar Leo's talk. I'm angry that the school teacher brother gave me a lesson when I asked him a good question.

"And the other one Paul gives us is also so simple. You see? It might not seem like anything at all. It has helped me through the most impossible times. It says 'If God is for us, who is against us?' Let's repeat that."

I won't repeat it. Because it's preposterous.

That question has three answers starting with the devil.

I'm going to tell that to the bald Little Friar Leo the first chance I get.

Cicero's Good Influence

When I get to my cell, a note is creased into the door jamb from a drunk who started to spell Cicero phonetically as you would 'sister,' then he realized that he couldn't reconcile the two 's' sounds in the middle. So he scribbled over the mistake, and ended with 'arrow.' Well I'm not going to call *Sis-arrow* because she didn't say it was urgent, and I don't want to be caught in the hallway phone booth if Origen walks by. The guy is possessed tonight.

To be fair, he wants to tell me something, and I haven't let him, because I know what he wants to say.

And I know what Cicero wants. She wants to know what I'm going to do about Odessa. I know what I'm going to do about Odessa: nothing.

I just haven't figured out how to tell Cicero that doing nothing means everything.

The important thing is that my trouble is solved, and now that I have been extracted from my dilemma, I can see where I was all bollixed up.

The issue was never whether I should be truthful with Cicero about the night with Odessa. The issue was not what Odessa would say about our secret now that she is as sick as she is.

The issue is whether I will protect Cicero from more injury. She hates her half sister enough as it is.

I got my answer through Origen: do no harm. It's especially important now that Marco is staying with us and I'm his dad in everything but name.

The anxiety that vexed me before is gone.

It occurs to me that I'm pacing this little Friar's cell the same way Charlie Gul paced at Quo Vadis, and I stop it, because I don't think like him anymore.

And it strikes me that I don't have to bring down Sodom in my ninth step confession to Cicero in order to tell her I'm sorry and ask her forgiveness. I don't need to ruin everything to get a clean start with my wife. I can tell Cicero about my general infidelities without burying myself in the grave particulars about Odessa. I don't know why this hasn't come to me sooner.

The Listerine with the 26.9 percent alcohol is still in the stupid medicine cabinet, and I walk to the window to see what the bell tower looks like under the moon, forgetting to stay clear of the window, because of who could be in the courtyard. It's too late. I smell his rising smoke.

"The savage moved to the cave, Byline," Ori's glowing. "He erected his fence against the animals and irrigated his field against the drought and sewed his skins against the cold."

The windowsill of my cell is flush with a mini radiator wide enough for me to sit on, and when I do, with my back to the bell tower, I look down at the moon glossing off Ori's pronounced forehead. Ori is not some scientist engaged in a clinical investigation about whether God's arm can reach the rejected, but a stage act, methodically working toward the point of dramatic accumulation where he will fall on his sword to prove that the love from above is no better than a placebo.

"He deployed his clan against the enemy and smoked his sacrifice against the demons. And when he was satisfied that he was protected, Byline, what did he do? He went to the *theater*."

"Good thing for Shakespeare."

"But the civilized man says, 'No. Let me control the *inside*.'"

"The reborn man you mean."

"Do what you have to do to make it fit your little theological deal, Byline, but there it is for you as clear as you could want it."

"I thought you said you were tired."

"Weary is what I said."

"That's two of us then." I regret coming to the window and I get up. He's going to try to reel me back.

"I don't envy you and your dilemma up there, Juliet."

There is it, and I don't buy it. He's not interested in my problem. I need to break this off quick. "If I don't sleep, I won't get up."

"That's what *He* said."

I don't buy that either. Ori isn't interested in a religion of resurrection or a God who died for runaways, except when it opens a path for Ori to preach heresy from his father the biochemist Leon Alexander.

Never again will Ori be the boy who gave the wrong answer 'blue' when his father asked him the color of the sky "*No, you idiot — that's the refraction you see — the sky is black.*" But Ori will always be the boy with his head pinned between his father's legs, the bones of the scientist's knees pressing his son's temple, trapping him in an everlasting moment of derision. His father thought it was funny. Ori remembers that — that and that his father touched him when he was a boy, or didn't touch him but did something *like* touching him that turned out to be the same thing. In whatever case, nobody touches Ori.

"You become a father, Byline, and you say one day 'Hey, wait a minute — I never wanted this *kid*,' but you can't shove him back up the portal, so you pour yourself into your work like my dad, or you run your little side shows like your old man did with the restaurants, but the kid knows — the kid always knows — that you're a killer. He doesn't have to wake up and see his old man standing over his bed with a pick."

Ori's talking about Pete the Breeze whose old man hit Pete in the head with an ice pick when he was six in his sleep. He told Pete something about a bug being on his head.

"Man's been a killer and a runner since Cain, Byline. That's why Brutus wants to twist you into a Greco-Roman pretzel. What's so funny?"

"What do you know about it?" He's talking about Odessa's father.

"About what Byline?"

"Wrestling."

"That there isn't much to know. You've got your entire theology based on the model of a father who has always been a murderer."

"I guess the point is to distinguish between the creature and the creator."

"Listen to me, Byline."

"Fatherhood is NOT the problem."

"This kid of Odessa's with your twinkle in his eyes."

"Shut up."

"Disconnection." Ori's enjoying this.

"He's got eyes of his own."

"We all do, Byline. That's the problem."

"Then let those with eyes see."

"If you could hear the deformity in your voice right now — "

"Yeah, what!"

"The sound of the Inquisition."

I slam the sash down hard enough to break the glass, but it doesn't crack. The rage inside me wants to drop great weight and smash Origen, but I back away, because abandonment hurts him worse.

If Ori is suggesting that I tell Cicero about Marco before he does, then this is a new game we're playing.

But that is not what Origen is saying, because you can't say what you don't know.

He's saying God can't reach the wounded, and so he wants out of here. Out of New York, and back to San Francisco where he went to film school and shot heroin with saboteurs and abused Cara Kole who made him the wicked wind in her third book of poetry. I've told him not to do that. The old neighborhood is death for a drunk.

The frustration for me is that Ori could believe in a God who saves if he would confront suffering with some courage, without tripping the traps of science, because when Origen falls, he falls on me. Cicero doesn't understand. She doesn't understand why I don't slam the window shut on him forever. I tell her over and over that faith in God is everything for a drunk. She says if God is so important, I should be trying to convert her.

I do try to convert her. And she knows it.

The yellow light falling through the closet door louvers makes shadow bars on the bed.

Ori is still looking up at my window — I feel the chill of his stare behind me — and for the first time, I wonder whether Ori would do anything dangerous if he stays in New York.

I should call Cicero. I should talk to her more often about everything that I think about when I think about her and Marco and the new baby coming and how it would be sweet, really sweet, if I could resurrect my dream restaurant. But it's late. And I have too many details to figure out.

I climb onto the thin bed and realize how odd it is to push my toes over a smooth, unruffled sheet without hitting panties or rolling a tee-shirt under my heel, or feeling the dried-hard spot of an otherwise soft washcloth under the heavy king-size comforter on our bed at home, where Cicero allows the stuff to accumulate. The bed gear admittedly does a good job of absorbing wet spots, and it is not as though Cicero lets it go rancid before she washes it, but I hold her habit against her the same way I hold her underwear against her, because she regards it as independence that I can't touch. Even now, after all I'm doing to prove myself changed.

She doesn't have a single article of normal intimate wear. She buys knickers in retro patterns from the Unique Shops on lower Broadway that look like Norman Rockwell checkerboard picnic cloths, or the petal-patterns from the non-slip stickers moms stuck on the floors of bathtubs in the 1960s. She's got these army-green khaki bras that are as thick as an overcoat and drain all the color out of her face, and wool half-corsets that she wears because they're warm, ignoring the yellowed sweat-stained crescents at the arms and back that don't wash out no matter how long you soak them.

The worst is the panties with the elastic that she rips out of the leg openings so that the material flaps like boxers, except they are much shorter than boxers and cut like bikinis, so that a flash of her hair mound or her white bottom has dangling before it little bits of broken thread stranded in the seams.

I don't even comment on them anymore.

She'll bleach black bras blue or red panties puke pink.

You look at her stunned sometimes.

She refuses to wear something that matches. Something with a little lace.

The only panties I liked — cute white ones with an embroidered match-box-size American flag raised off the right cheek — I've never seen again. She brought them home the day she cut her hair so short it was spiked at the temples. The point is, what do you say when your wife wears pre-owned tie-died underwear to bed? Bleached through the elastic, of course, to set your heart at ease about what manner of hippie romp these openings must have seen before you: 'Oh girl, I'm really in the mood now?' No. That's the point. It's a head-butt. Bed politics. It's Andy Warhol. It isn't art. It's anti-art. You want to see some beauty? Well guess what, sucker? There is none.

I want the girl back with the big black bag and the wet penny-blonde hair who tricked a Virginia trucker out of his wad and introduced me to her breasts ten minutes after we used his money to share a hotel room in Bethlehem. She walked out of the bathroom in two mini towels, one tied on her hips and the other wrapping her head, with enough water on her shoulders to streak what she just dried. I shocked myself back to attention and laughed, because that was a hell of a greeting.

I was in Bethlehem to make sure I was still going east. There was Cicero at the pay phone, vibrating the way she does when she's desperate, her lips thin with tightness, saying 'I want his rocks' while she dug into the half-peeled roll of quarters to beat the beep-beep-beep prompt for more money. I spied in long enough to understand that she was trying to reach a woman who was with Cissy's dad when he died, and that Cicero was going to drive to Canada that night to 'find' her unless this person on the phone was more helpful. I laughed because Canada is a big place and Cicero didn't look like the methodical type. She heard me having fun and spun around, jabbing her middle finger towards me, losing the quarter she was trying to get, and then the telephone call.

She looked like one of those girls in college sitting alone at the bend of the bar who you don't approach, because something about the way she stares at you reminds you of your inadequacy as a contender.

I've never been afraid of girls like that. And I laughed again in disbelief when I saw Cicero was going to blame me for losing the call.

"Don't take money from anyone here," I told her. I could tell she had been pretty her whole life and had paid for it.

I told her to forget about her dad and this woman who was on the boat with him when it caught fire, and the stupid jewelry that he was supposed to leave Cicero in his will.

"You don't want his rocks," I told her.

"The one thing that was mine and he gave them to *her*," she said. By this point, Cicero was crying streaks into her mascara.

"He left you in good shape. Look at you."

But she wasn't listening.

She was bent over with her head in the bathroom sink, giving away the entire shape of her bottom in stretched jeans to any jerk who would peer past the open doorway into the long mirror.

I felt bad for her that her dad was a dead dog, and that Cicero had made herself so vulnerable with the water running down her hair into the drain off the Pennsylvania Turnpike.

I saw in her that night a look like she knew something was going to happen. She looked like she had never been young. She looked like she always understood her dreams, but had no concept of mystery.

The next night we dripped Angostura bitters between her legs, and Cicero sat up and said she would deny it if I ever repeated it, which made me laugh, because if I was going to repeat anything about this girl, it would be that she had peed the hotel bed so bad the night before that my *pillow* was wet.

In fact, those first Manhattan nights on York Avenue when Cicero would try to drink the way I did, she peed like a disobedient dog. One morning after we fought and I found my black uniform trousers wet with warm piss, I told Charlie Gul why I was wearing jeans behind the bar. It's one of those things C-Gul knows that becomes more expensive with each gain I make sober.

I've forgotten to pray my night prayer, and I'm too settled to get out of bed now and hit my knees. God won't mind this one time if I don't get up, move the twelve inches from this bed to the floor, and kneel.

Prayer isn't about posture, it's about a person, as the retreat leader said at dinner.

I say my prayer from here. I thank God for removing my desire for a drink or a drug today, and for putting people in my path who helped me, and for extricating me from my unbelievable dilemma. And I ask God to show me where I have been wrong in the last 24 hours — where I have been selfish and self-seeking. And I see as my day rewinds a fast-forward image of Cissy with folded bare legs, sitting at our kitchen table on Sunday when I'm due home, waiting for the truth. Anguished when I don't give it to her. It cuts me where I thought I was protected.

But how could that be *my* wrong? I must be seeing my own invention. I know God's will is that I do no harm. God has made that clear to me. So why point me to this bad scene of conviction?

Maybe I have pointed myself to it.

I don't like this at all. I get out of bed and hit my knees and start over.

This time I don't see Cicero when I go over my 24 hours. I don't see anyone except the school teacher brother, who I left in a rude way, and Ori, who's been trying to tell me something. This is more like what I expect, but it is also a pain because now that I've seen it, I have to make it up to them both.

I'm just glad I don't have to confront Odessa.

In the hushglow of sleep, a dream dawns in blue, and I am seated on a bentwood cane chair, looking at the uncovered wood tables that we would clear for the after-hours drinkers at Quo Vadis. Everything is screened blue: the dark hardwood floor with the wide, uneven boards, the brick wall with framed mirrors that reflect metallic powder light, and the sets of votive candles flicker-dancing on the tables. The people who have filled up the dining room and crowded the bar are the same dusk skyscape color, and the tint of their foreheads and cheeks and bare shoulders is blue-rose. The light that drops from the ceiling as though I have the front line table at a dinner theater has a steamy shimmer to it.

I would know that I was dreaming for sure were it not for Charlie Gul at Table 6 with the model corps, wagging his cigarette at me.

It occurs to me that I am smoking, too. And drinking a pink gin from the New Yorker coffee cup I had behind the bar at Quo Vadis. Brutus Cruz is leading 24 West Point cadets in a push-up drill with their shirts off and my mother, in her old Gamma Delta sweatshirt from Southern Illinois University, is reading from one of her letters to me, which I never answer, because they are loaded with more scripture than a Sunday sermon. She is saying "If he won't read them I will," and the recruits sound off "Amen!" with each push off the floor.

Odessa finger-straddles two vodka martinis in 8-ounce wine glasses with her left hand as only she was allowed to do, in a restaurant where everything was served off trays. Her skirt rides up the hump of her darkened backside, and she swings her hair into my face and says, 'Cicero wants to know what you're doing here.' Cicero is baby-sitting my grown sister Jackie who is crying because she doesn't 'get' her math homework and she has a test in the morning, and I can hear the echoes of my drunk father in the kitchen "Why do we even do it anyway? They want their food? *You* give it to them." He means me. But I can't help my sister finish her math or help my father get the food out or help Origen refine his thesis about Agency and Empathy, which he has laid out in blue-black spiral notebooks on the table next to me, because I'm thinking that if I don't finish this pink gin, it will not technically be a drink, and I will not have to start the AA program over.

Starting over is an impossible thought to think.

They're laughing at the bar because they've got some chick drunk past caring, but someone is shouting the equivalent of fire and I can't make out what the mob wants, coming straight at me. A soldier in uniform with a dark blue beret is marching into the light in front of me with a naked girl slug over his shoulder, dead or not conscious, with her hair almost touching the floor and her bottom cleft sewn up from surgery, from her tail bone to her vagina. The sutures are as thick as twine and laced like seams on a football. It looks fresh and bloody with dark rose-blue blotches at the skin punctures, and scars of crusted blue blood in the cavity between her dark lifeless thighs.

"Who is responsible for this!" The soldier is shouting like a cop who knows the answer but wants a confession. "Who is responsible for this!"

Everyone is dread serious except C-Gul, who is laughing because I have taken another drink and blown my sobriety, laughing at me for trying to live the fantasy life off booze.

I don't know anything, except this is an abortion. I don't know this girl or this guy in the beret, but I'm as angry as he is for the girl and I take over the shout, "Who is responsible for this!"

But when I say it, no one wants to know.

When I say it, the gravity disappears.

The girl with the bloody-blue sewn up anal cleft is gone. So are the people at the bar and the butcher Brutus Cruz and my wife and my mother and sister and old man with the voice from Hell's kitchen. Origen is also leaving.

He turns his back on me so I won't hear it but I hear it anyway: "Who else, Byline?"

The Voice in the Garden

I awake unable to shake that bad dream — not so much the guilt of drinking gin again, but the enduring image of that awful stitched-up bottom — so that not even the cool pines outside or this late August sun streaking into my window relieve me.

Every drunk in recovery has drunk dreams. Drunk dreams make you feel unclean, but you get over them once they lose their fire of surprise.

This was more than a drunk dream.

I leave the cell without my boots, the way St. Francis did it, but as I walk out of the Enclosure and see the statue of the little beggar, I'm suddenly self-conscious about my bare feet, and I hope no one who sees me thinks I'm showing off more than I am.

Coffee is supposed to be in the prayer garden before the morning meeting, and there is still a smoky mist in the green river valley to the

West. The old Friary from the outside has the smooth gray stucco face of a European river village, with petite square windows that push into the roofline, and a second row of dormer windows with arched tops and slate shingles, spaced with chocolate-brown Tudor strips.

The moment I become attuned to the heavy-pipe wind chimes in the prayer garden downhill, my ears burn with the thought that I should have answered my mother's last letter.

I only saw my mother once in Europe when we met in Amsterdam, but I was so stoned on black hash that I remember only an older woman behind an unwiped plate glass window in the Red Light District, dancing with a gold-tasseled rope. The way my mind would betray me afterwards, I couldn't separate my mother's face from that vile dancer.

It occurs to me as my ears cool that the only person who didn't confront me in that bad dream last night was my old man, who's in Belgium.

A missing act from the beginning.

My father was making $100,000 at *The Granier* in St. Louis when my mother first knew him, but by the time I was born they had busted him down to a sous chef, making under $1,000 a week. My mother had found gravlax and foi gras in the basement and fought with him about where he got it, until the day in second grade when my enemies at school showed me in the newspaper where Adamo Dante had been charged with felony larceny. He denied to me that he did it even much later in Chicago. They found capon and caviar in our basement refrigerator, but they never found the cognac or the champagne. After that, my father never worked full time.

My mom was still crying over him when she left the states.

The lesson there, of course, is to fall in love poor. That way, there ain't so far to drop.

The cherry wood entrance over the stairwell of the prayer garden is set below the sloping street level, so that you have to duck to pass under it. The rock wall is 12 feet high where they excavated to keep the garden level, even as everything else goes downhill, and the pond in the middle is hemmed with round field stones. Someone with skill has taken care to build a red wooden foot bridge, arched over the center like a bucket handle. A large stone cherub squirts water out of his mouth into a pool of pancake-sized lily pads, and a bullfrog heats in the sun that beats through the dark purple leaves of a young maple.

I don't know where I got the idea there would be coffee here. I must be losing my mind. I was picturing a bagel and bacon as well.

A black pond lizard is not afraid of me on the walkway, and there is an old cement bench near a shed-size greenhouse where I am going to sit and cry. I feel it coming on. I don't know why.

The brothers planted rosemary and thyme in an old claw-foot bathtub, painted robin-egg blue. Each new birdhouse I encounter makes me forget how distinct the last one was, and I'm fascinated by the order and variety that these simple plants provide in the white morning sun.

I stop at an ivy-covered St. Francis shrine, with petitions stuck between his arm and chest. A plaque dedicates it to "All those affected by AIDS and to all the Men and Women in Recovery. Do Not Fear to Hope."

I don't need a reason to cry, because it's coming anyway, but this pushes me past my limit.

It's the same remorse that hit me when I ran into Danny the Dreamer my first night in AA, and the Dreamer said "So, have you had enough?"

Yeah. I'd had enough then.

And I've had enough now.

Enough of this second chance I never asked for and don't deserve. Enough of a magnanimous God who deems a deathbed turn to Him more important than a lifetime of willful diversions. Enough of this peace in spite of everything I've done to kill it.

Mucus as thin as water runs out my nostrils and over my lip, and the breath I expel in spasms is hot from the pot of my distress. I see a human head out of my blind side, and I look right with my wet face to the shaded sun, even though I know that it is not a figure but a figment that has appeared before when I cry.

I can't see out of my blind eye.

I have no reason to stop this fist of tears, this swelling of my heart over everything I can't control. I am 27 years old, and I have known God too late. I have spent my life avoiding this moment. This vulnerability and self-weakness and begging. This knowledge that I am dependent on a God who is too pure to be touched or seen. A God too good to be real.

It feels as though I'm being watched by a stadium of faces, and the comfort of their company quiets the rushing fluids in my head. It feels as though they approve not of me or my sobbing but of my weakness.

Coolness returns to my breath, and the pond lizard darts into the shrine ivy.

On the hard bench under the lilac, I try what the Little Friar Leo suggested last night about imagining yourself seated in the hand of God when you pray.

But when I close my eyes, I see a hand — huge and unnatural — and then I see the roseflesh-blue bottom of the girl in the dream.

This isn't working. I was closer to God in my tears. And I go back to the regret and the self-pity and the sorry feeling of undeserved grace. Now I see the flashes of my past: my cracked up Delta 88, the gums and red teeth where the Henry Hudson Parkway pavement ripped the cheek off Odessa, the horror in Emily Cruz's eyes when she woke up and saw me masturbating over her, the blackness in my mind's sight like a night of solid blood on my 21st birthday when Odessa blinded me.

The blackness in my mind's sight that has never left.

You think you'll be young forever and you'll never lose your mind's edge, and if your time in front of the world doesn't come today, it's only because your debut is waiting for a more glorious entrance, when you will emerge higher, larger and smarter. But you don't get any smarter, only cheaper. And you don't get your time on stage, only a longer view of your old lines that you threw away. The world knows your act is about telling others what to do, and no one wants to hear that.

So I don't know anything that I thought I knew, and I haven't learned the way on my own, because I'm no better than the bad I was before. My way wanted me dead. But You saved me for your way. To die each day. Is that your way? Speak to me, Lord.

My head fills with the noise of the enemy: Cicero tapping her fingers at the kitchen table, unsure about the baby after all, Brutus practicing his take downs in the MacArthur gym at West Point, Origen hawking his car and buying a plane ticket to San Francisco to bleed on Cara Kole and drop into the Bay, hitting the water red as he's always dreamed.

I don't know why I listen for God's voice in my heart as though I expect something audible, but if other people can hear him, I have to believe I can. I don't have a choice but to believe. It's like everything else today: all my hope rides on things I've never seen.

I have no eye anymore. I have no bar. I have no bottle or hash pipe or Porticoes with the mental lay stations where any girl I imagined from here to St. Louis I could commandeer into low positions. I have no freedom but the self-examined way.

It's as hard as bricks.

Speak, Lord, because if you don't, I'm a dead, dry drunk.

The pond lizard has leaped on a grape leaf that stems back to a wooden arbor, dedicated to Little Friar Leo from the Matt Talbot 7s.

The vines are too young for fruit. Maybe they're sterile. Maybe they're poisoned. They could be false vines. Or maybe they're cursed. Whatever the problem, they ought to have growth if they stay grounded. If they stay in the light.

Again I shut my eyes against the temptress Odessa, and my nose against the sewer of C-Gul, and my ears against the footsteps of an Inn Man trodding the road above.

I say my mantra against it all. "Speak, Lord."

Then I hear in me as clear as church bells: "Give Up Your Picture."

It sounds like my inner voice but it's not my word choice.

I'm sure I heard it right, because I can't decide what to think of it.

If what I think happened just happened, I'm delivered. But I'm not about to be fooled. So I wait.

I wait to see if there is anything more to come. What more would there be? This is it.

I'm too excited and stirred up to wait quietly. I rewind my memory and listen to the words to be sure I heard them right. I know that I did. "Give Up Your Picture."

This is a big deal. It's bigger than me, yet it's been given to me. Give up my picture.

What picture, that's the question.

I'm looking around the garden for help — a bird, a brother, an Inn Man — because this message is huge news. And it could mean more than one thing.

If I could just decide on one thing that it means, that would be good.

But it's no good. Nothing comes to me this way.

I need to move to think.

When I get back to my cell I write it in the margin of the orange bulletin, and I'm convinced of its authenticity. I keep daring the words to fail under scrutiny. But they're both modest and profound. Also a bit vague. It only convinces me more that this is not some interior invention, because I don't speak to myself in oracles.

I write it again on the flyleaf of my AA Big Book, and it looks more decided still, then I go back to the front door and pick up another note that Cicero called. This time the message-taker misspelled my name: "Dontay," it's written. "Call your wife."

Cicero's angry.

What I really need to do is stay focused and figure out this picture. I never should have left the garden. I should have taken the moment to ask for an interpretation. The sooner I get Cissy off my back, the sooner I can go back to the garden.

I'm two steps into the hall with my quarters when I see Origen plodding towards me with the heat of the morning sun from the porch window behind him riding on his back.

Cissy answers on the first ring as though it's an emergency, but I know that it isn't. She wants to know why I didn't call her last night. I get no hello or anything, and I immediately put on half ears with her, listening for the catchwords that explain the urgency.

When she asks me if I'm listening, I say: "I was out praying."

"I need you to come home now, Baby."

I don't say anything because Cissy exaggerates before she gives you her bottom line. If Marco was sick or the doctor said something about the baby, Cissy would have told me first thing, and I'm not about to ask her why she's all hyper-boiled this time, because it would only dignify her tactic.

Ori has his neon-green spiral notebook that he uses for notes about the human genome. A pencil is wedged between his low ear and his tremendous temple.

"Are you listening?" She says.

"Yes," I tell her again, although she must know I'm not listening. "What do you want me to say? There's a day-and-a-half left that I already paid for."

"I told you O.D. is sick and I need help with Marco."

Odessa is sick. What's that supposed to be, news?

Cicero doesn't need help with Marco. I doubt the kid even knows I'm gone.

Cissy has more non-emergencies than a 911 switchboard in Scarsdale. Origen in his dark shades has wandered into my blind field and picked up on the conversation.

"Your mom and Brutus can't come?" I ask her.

"Don't call him that."

It kills Cicero that I call the major Brutus, because Ori gave him the nickname; Cicero doesn't like Brutus any more than I do.

"Baby, I *told* you they're with her at the hospital."

There's Cissy's bottom line. Now I am thinking Odessa is sick.

"I called you last night. I needed you to come home. And now you're arguing with me."

"Look, girl — "

"No, Baby, you come home."

I mean to tell Cicero that this retreat has meant great grace for me. I want to make her understand that this isn't some degenerate weekend with the boys I'm on, but a communion with God that can't be rushed.

I contemplate telling her about the voice in the garden but my attention leaps to Origen, who is talking to me like a spoiled Westchester 5-year-old when his mom is on the phone, and I think, *'What's this maniac want?'* It doesn't matter. Cissy's hung up.

"Disconnection. The one thing you can depend on." Ori's lips curl into a brown smile. His breath is as smoky as ash.

"She wants me to come home."

"They all do, Byline, but no one has since Ulysses."

"Odessa is sick."

"Yeah, well they've known about the CD4 receptor all along now but there's this other pier on the T-lymphocyte that loops through the membrane, and *that* is how the virus is docking up. Once the HIV empties its machinery into the T-cell and you get the reverse transcriptase hand shake to convert the RNA, you're off to races. The whole thing is ingenious."

I'm thinking that if Odessa is sick and back in ICU, there's no way I could visit her, much less ask Odessa if we can adopt Marco.

I couldn't hope for a more genuine solution to my dilemma.

But I don't like leaving the holy mountain before my time.

I just can't think, trapped in this box, how to call Cissy back and argue my way out of going home.

"They blow smoke up your ass talking about this vaccine because every infected cell is a mutant. That's the problem with AZT. But these cocktails that mess with polypeptide sequence are the real deal. Tragedy she didn't hang on for the *pro-tease* inhibitors. If you know what I mean."

He's playing on words because he's stuck on the one-dimensional image of Odessa as a nymph, and I brush past to my room.

"Her T-cells are 80," I tell him. "Her coffin will be a shoebox."

"Depends on what T-cells you mean, Byline. If you don't know, you're in over your head."

"You wanna bag the biochemistry lesson?"

"Microbiology. You're going? It's only Saturday."

"I don't know what I'm doing. I got a kid at home who needs help."

"Telemachus can wait a day. He's waited this long."

Ori worships Joyce and Shakespeare. Shakespeare is his paternal spirit. Stephen Dedalus is Ori's prophet. I don't care which one he's referring to. It amounts to the same.

He's saying he knows something that he doesn't know.

I sling my black bag over my shoulder.

"Look. I know you want to talk about going to San Francisco, but I thought you were going to pray about it."

"No *you* look, kid. You want to damn everyone outside your church and coupon me with your exhortation to prayer so you can go home where the bed is warm — well, two can act this one out. There's nothing for me here. I'm looking at the proof! I'm going to do it, Byline. I'm going to Frisco."

"Save the plane fare and cut your balls off here."

"Good idea."

"Buy a vase for them."

"Even better. A libation with olives."

"Your problems will jump right on the plane with you. What the hell are you going to do in San Francisco?"

"Frisco isn't Nirvana, Byline. New York is hell. I told you. I got the *tire*."

He means the tractor-trailer truck tire that snapped off its axle on the Catskills Parkway last week and sailed toward his windshield like a millstone of judgment to smite him, except for a miracle change in the tire's midair trajectory. The tire wound up bouncing a foot behind his brake lights and into the woods, but Ori insists it was God's warning for him to get out of New York. I told him it was the positive opposite. God missed Ori purposely to show him mercy.

Through the window, giant pines bend in the high-altitude wind, and I realize that I'm miscast in this hand-to-starving-man role. The role belongs to Cara Kole, but she can't take it. Cara Kole's father raped her. Ori's father razed him. Neither of the two suspected the other's bad dad past, except in their unspoken treaty to repeat the abuse. So Ori left her. And Cara Kole left him. And there is no getting Cara Kole back because like a caracole she is perpetually shelled up in her hideaway, sinking her center deeper inside, even as she reaches out for someone new.

And Cara Kole is okay with that.

She will always be okay with that, as long as nobody touches her.

Ori is blocking my way out of here. He's not serious about castration, because it would represent a *change*, and God knows if Ori changed, it would sack his thesis.

So I tell him: "You're not the prophet out of the desert who tells everybody the truth about themselves."

"Fine, Byline. You want the part, take it."

"Cut off your balls because you're disgusted when you jack off or because you want to punish Cara Kole, but have the guts to admit why you're doing it and drop this high purpose."

"The Good Samaritan is allegory, Byline. Wake up! People look at me and they cross to the other side because if they stopped they might see their own dread. No one wants to get in range because once they saw the horror in their own mirror, and they're still running from it!"

"If I thought there was nothing better for me sober than what I had drinking and drugging with the Cords of Falsehood — "

"Then you'd be an island instead of a long distance runner."

"Then I would *drink*."

"But Byline, we wouldn't get to see Act III." His forehead is enormous with the contortion of his burden.

"Out of my way," I tell him.

"They have treated the wounds of my people carelessly, saying peace, peace when there is no peace!"

He's using scripture on me, and for just a second it divides my resolve to put him behind me and get out of here, because God speaks through anyone.

But Ori is violating the silence rule, shouting after me down the Enclosure, and that cancels my obligation to listen to him.

I just hope my Parisienne starts so I can get out of here.

"Don't ask and don't tell is for birds of the air, Byline!" He's shouting like a daylight Bowery act. "They'll separate you from your bones!"

"Shut up!" I whisper so harshly that my throat feels like it's full of sand. "Shut your mouth!"

"Don't do it, Byline."

Book Two

DISCLOSURE

Faithful Cohabitation

Our barn-red bungalow looks no different beneath the unsettled sky.

I expected to see Brutus Cruz's Humvee blocking our driveway, or some sign of the emergency Cicero touted to call me off the holy mountain with Origen a day early, but there is nothing unusual about our little house on the ridge, except that Marco has left his turtle cage open at the curb. Tut-Tut has been dropped on his shell too many times to rig his own escape. I'm sure Marco has him in the woods.

The clouds have invaded the sky without a fight, and it's fifteen degrees darker in just the moment it's taken me to look into the kitchen windows for Cicero.

I sit on the porch steps with my back to the door and wait for Marco.

The ridge in our backyard woods drops 160 feet to the railroad tracks and the electrified third rail, and it strikes me now that Cissy is right — the kid is too young to be in there by himself. But I don't get up to go after him. I pray that he'll come out. I don't want to cross the yard where Cissy will see me from the bedroom window.

I need to know what's going on first.

I sense Marco in the wind before I see him. Mop top hair and brown knees pumping, he holds Tut-Tut like a sandwich in his hands. Marco has not been in the woods at all but on the landlord's side of the house where he knows not to go. Our landlady, Boer, has an emphysemic 40-year-old son who is too weak to mow grass, shovel snow, or lift anything heavier than the phlegm from his sick lungs each morning at the 5:30 hacking hour. It's never occurred to me until now to fence the yard in myself.

Marco is the double image of the peasant boy with the rain-puddle eyes in the 1955 film, *Marcelino Pan y Vino*, except for the pan Asian cheek line he gets from Odessa.

"You know to stay away from the Boer side," I tell him. He isn't listening because I haven't *made* him listen the way I should as a father. "Come here, Marco!"

He's headed for the street with his eyes to the ground, not looking ahead of him. Something unspoken from inside me goes out to him and fills the space between us. A cloud as heavy as Gideon's fleece pulls up under the sun. I pray that he will stop before he hits the street, because my shout won't stop him.

And he does stop at the cage. He tucks at the waist, and down drops his turtle into the wire box. The lizard's shell thuds against the bar wire as Marco drags it back across the grass.

"Did you see your Mommy?" I stand up to show him it would only take me two steps to handle him. He was going to pass me again.

"No."

"You didn't see your Mommy?" Cicero made it sound like they were all at the hospital.

"She doesn't feel good."

"Did you talk to her?"

"I don't feel like saying."

That's his mother Odessa talking. And she isn't sick. Not the way Cicero made it out. I can tell.

"Do it anyway," I tell him. "Did you talk to her last night?"

"No. When I woke up. Are you going to bring me to the pool?"

"Not today. Where's Aunt Cissy?"

"Can we go to the pool please?"

"Look. It's going to rain. If that cloud was any heavier we'd have to build a boat. What's she doing in there?"

"We can go and if it rains we can get out."

"Is she upstairs?"

"I'm right here." Cicero's voice is smoother and cooler than it was on the telephone. I can see her white throat through the upstairs screen.

"This is the help you need?" I ask her.

"You said you were coming right home."

"That's what you said. I'm looking for the crisis."

"You think I would lie?"

Marco tries to escape.

“Where are you going?” I shout. “I don’t want you in the woods by yourself anymore.”

Marco stops as though he’s really going to listen, but he doesn’t look over his shoulder at me, because he knows where the crisis is.

Cissy is on her way down, and I’ll be the one in the fire before I can make the kid mind me.

So I threaten him: “What happened last night? Did you give your Aunt Cissy a hard time?”

He’s not going to answer. He’s too smart. He knows my clock is running out.

I beat through the door and into the kitchen because I have a feeling Marco wasn’t the only one acting up last night.

My sauté pans are hanging out of size sequence. I told Cicero if she uses them to hang them back in order.

And my best knife wet in the sink!

“Look, Baby!” She starts in on me without a warm up from the living room threshold. “Why should I beg to see my own husband?”

“What’s this?” I stop her advance by flashing the Wusthof blade to show her that it’s been wet overnight.

“What are you doing?”

“Saving it, girl. In spite of you. Since when do you need my Wusthof to make macaroni and cheese?”

“Are you guessing what my night was like?”

“Leave my stuff alone. It’s expensive. I told you. What’s this! Do I need to lock it up?” She must have used two ounces of my saffron.

“Why do we even have it?”

“You used *half* of it. On what! Are you out of your mind?”

"You didn't call me back. I knew you better when you drank. You make me feel guilty when I want you to stay home because AA is so important but you *like* sharing your feelings with all your single women!"

"Who are you fooling?"

I'm the one who told her that Alcoholics Anonymous is degenerating into a singles scene.

"You'd rather help Origen than your own wife. Tell everyone how happy you make me sober and saved! I'm so happy I'm walking out the door!"

"The guy wants to castrate himself, girl."

"Who cuts his penis off?"

"His balls. His balls."

"It's so much more normal to cut off your testicles than your penis! What kind of sicko does that?"

"There's little thing called 'work while there's still light'."

"You have a pregnant wife and little boy in your house! What light are you talking about? You're on a pink cloud!"

Cicero has something behind her back, and the only reason she's stopped stabbing me with her tongue is she's timing how to bring it out.

Her breasts drape wide of her ribs because both shoulders are pinned back, still holding whatever it is in ambush.

Her thighs twitch in her white denim skirt.

That's where the cheap shots are coming from. Cicero's about to gamble here, so she throws the dirt to improve her odds.

She's the infidel. She's the one who was writing 'Cicero Stone' in her daybook, fantasizing what it would be like to take the name of that dentist in the Bronx with the vibrator in his office. The vibrator and the turn-of-the century articles about the female massage technique that could cure hysteria and depression. He told Cicero he had a friend with a clinic in Barbados who was doing root canal on women using nothing but vibrators. Cicero says she never believed it, but I say she did. She liked his two-eyed attention and the fact he didn't drink. Cicero thought by telling me about him it would bring us closer. Ha! It incensed me.

I hate the whole Bronx because of him.

I'm ready for what she's got. I'm so ready that my mind wanders back to the holy mountain.

"What are these?" She's got white panties balled up in her fist. They're hers.

"They're yours."

"Where'd they come from?"

"The Unique?"

"You remember them." She's nodding as though we're both on script.

"I do."

I've given the wrong answer. I see her displeasure in the arc of her nostrils. It's the same look she had the morning she showed me the bills in bed that fell out of my pocket. They were on her side of the bed, actually. And she was treating me like the dog's nose in its own mess. She had the wild idea that I meant it as a tip.

"Try again, Baby."

She's holding the underwear contemptuously with her thumb and forefinger now, the raised-thread American flag stiff on the soft cotton folds, and her own breasts hardened like the turtle's shell.

"I have a better plan." I slide my Wusthof into the knife block. "There's no crisis here."

"Want one?"

"Who are you threatening?"

"Who are you smiling at? Do these look like I would buy them?"

"That's why I liked them."

"Do I sew?"

"What?" Honestly. What does sewing have to do with it? "I don't know. Do I sing?"

"You don't sing, and I don't sew." She says it from so low in her throat that it sounds woeful. And now I have an awful thought that Ori called her. "You did it, didn't you, Baby."

I don't know what she's talking about, but if this is an ambush, I'm the one with the surprise. She wants to know the truth? She can have the facts. I'll do my 9th step amends with her right here.

"I wasn't planning on doing my amends with you today, you know. There's a better way."

Somehow now we both know that I'm going to do it anyway.

I look at the empty baker's rack in the corner, as tall as the refrigerator, and I wonder how I ever got so excited about picking it up on auction. I mean, there are 16 tray grooves on that damn thing. When was I going to use it? It was just a crutch to keep my restaurant dream alive.

The reality is that Cissy has stuffed her clothes into every baseboard cabinet in the kitchen, and her case studies are buckling the pantry shelves. It was all supposed to be temporary. There was a day she wouldn't dream of intruding on my kitchen space. Now I notice something else — a celery-colored Annie Hall hat hanging in the reflection of the bathroom mirror. Hats are the devil for a man's wife. What's she going to do next, pull out her scarves from college, or go get groceries without a bra?

A red flag. Maybe this *is* the time to get it all out. "You know," I tell her. "I was always drunk and stoned at Quo Vadis."

"And?" She's hyper-annoyed.

"And they were always doing lines," I tell her. "It was always after two-thirty when I had done the money and locked the doors and the Spanish were making their rice and eggs in the back, thinking Charlie Gul didn't know. I'm not blaming this on the booze, okay? I'm just saying what it was. It was always Thursday night when they would come in. I didn't know names for most of them. It wasn't about that. I'm not talking about hands-on anything with any of them except what I did in my head and a little stand up make-out on the tiles with Carmen when she was upset with Domo."

"Do I know about the tiles?"

"Outside by the loading dock where the break tables were."

"With Carmen."

"It was in my head what I did with them that was wrong. You know what I mean? Are you listening to me?"

She's looking out the window with folded arms.

The pale yellow sky has a sick look that it will vomit at any moment.

"Marco should be in here," I tell her. "You and I should be at a restaurant talking about this, the way it's meant to be done, and I would be sorry and answer all your questions, instead of arguing with this stupid underwear in my face because you called me home from a prayer retreat so you could do what?"

"I want to hear everything." She won't look at me. "Every night I was alone missing you, thinking about you, wondering what to do with myself and trying to look good for you when you got home so that you would say something nice or wake me up once. Did you love Carmen?"

"You know Domo screwed around on Carmen as soon as she left the restaurant. I was the only one who didn't lie to her."

"Poor girl. Good for you. What a pair. Is that it?"

"What."

"Girls with no names who you didn't touch every night for three years and giving Carmen what she needed. This is my big ninth step?"

"I'm telling you. It's embarrassing. It wasn't *this.*" I show her the cup of my hand to mimic a backside grab, and then I tap my head. "It was *this.*"

"Just say it."

"Everything inside me was an open sewer."

"Fantasies?"

"Porn."

"These are perfect for you then." She means the underwear, but she hasn't unclenched them. She's preoccupied. Otherwise she would be out of breath with red vibration, interrogating me.

"I know he called you," I tell her.

She turns to face me in an aggressive little pose, jutting her copper-flecked forehead under the pool table lights we hung above the butcher block. Her freckles glisten where the hair gel has spotted them.

"What are you going to tell me?"

There's only one thing she could be talking about. This is the same conversation we had yesterday about asking Odessa if we could adopt Marco before she dies. An impossible risk.

"Didn't we just have this conversation? Didn't we decide I'd go to the mountain and be sure about this going to Odessa stuff so we wouldn't get blown with chaff in the wind like some dentist and his vibrator?"

"Like you and O.D!"

It didn't faze her. I nailed Cicero with that crack and she still flew straight at me. She's obsessed with the Odessa question.

They say in the Program that 'No' is a complete sentence. So I tell her "No."

"No?" She's on her feet with the underwear balled in her fist again. The column of her neck is straight as a pillar.

Stick debris flies past the window frame, and the pea-green sky heaves with distress.

"Use your brain, girl. How am I going to get into the ICU to see her?"

"This is why I called you home." She's shaking her head, twisting her Inca sun earrings against their anchors.

"What did Ori say!"

"I knew this wouldn't work! You weren't praying. You were hiding! You were never going to tell me, were you?"

"Tell you what, girl!"

"About O.D! About Marco! About these! Do you still love her?"

The panties drop off my chest after clinging there, falling to the boots of my infidelity.

The first feet of rain hit the roof with a rattling march. The background light through the window is overrun with awful gray mess.

"Do you still love her, damn it!"

I don't know what to do right now, but I have to pick my sight up off the panties.

My throat seizes, and the conversation I had with Charlie Gul the night he came through the Porticoes fills my ears: *'How many times?'* 'I don't know. A lot.' *'What did she do*?' 'She did everything.' *'She communicated.'* 'Yeah. She was a great communicator.'

Cicero must know, despite her anguish, that I never loved Odessa.

Odessa and I didn't talk.

Everything with Odessa was surface flirt and high school hallway eye games. Something to do on the pink gin and the PCP and the low life after three. I never said a word to Odessa, so she could keep alive what hope she had, and Odessa didn't say much to me, so that I could do the same, but instead of liking myself more when I was with her, I hated who I was.

When she figured that out, it made her feel selfish and cruel. I know it because that's what she called me the night she blinded me.

People don't despise things in others that they haven't already loathed in themselves.

I must be shaking my head back and forth.

"You're going like this but no words come out." Cissy's mocking me. Behind her it's as black as midnight. "I asked you why you did it."

I look down to the kitchen carpet and then instinctively up again, because I can't be servile anymore. I just can't.

I look at Cicero's knee with the violet fishhook scar from the fire escape fall.

The stinging around my heart is relentless. Damn, I didn't see this coming! Damn Origen Alexander! Damn everyone from the Program to the holy mountain who saved my neck for this high noon hanging.

"If I told you, you wouldn't believe it."

"I believe anything, don't I."

"So you take his word for it."

"Who?"

"Origen."

"What does this have to do with Origen!"

"Why else would you accuse me?"

"Because she never talked about the father, Bobby! Not once."

Cicero's answer disarms the defense I was building and pulls the noise of the storm into the kitchen.

I don't dare face her. Not even now that Marco has burst in out of breath, asking for his boots and pirate ship.

We don't have his ship here, and the last time I couldn't raise my head and face my accuser like this, I was drinking.

"What are those, Bub?" Marco couldn't be more serious. The little guy couldn't be more hopelessly, cluelessly serious.

He has walked in from a world turned black to an aunt so rocked that she couldn't smile at him as she ran by, and a half-blind uncle he calls Bub with women's underwear at his feet.

And hearing the sweet tone of the boy try to understand his world makes me long for my innocence. No wonder Adam was banished for despising it. His unfaithful wife with him.

If I don't watch it, I'm going to cry.

"What are those, Bub?"

"If I knew I wouldn't be here."

"Put them in the hamper."

"Do you know about these?"

"No."

"What about this?" I show him the flag up close.

"No."

"Of course not. Come here. I'll show you a secret about the rain."

On the porch we keep our backs to the red clapboard siding because the wind is spraying the rain up to our feet. I see that Marco has found the one dry spot behind the tomato planter to park his armored lizard.

"What secret?"

"You have to watch. You have to watch the ground for a spot with something dark behind it. There by the tree trunk. See how hard it's coming down. See that?"

"No."

"Look by the car. The back tire. See how fast that's coming down? Have you ever seen anything move like that?"

"That's not a secret. A secret is something you can't tell."

"Well, I got news for you –"

"This is dumb."

"We haven't gotten to the good part."

"It's not a secret."

"Then why did you come out here? Without your boots? Listen. You have to get your body quiet. Then you'll hear. That's the secret."

For a second in the pounding-down shower, I think I hear Cicero howling. But it's my right ear. Ever since Odessa blinded me, I get crying in my right ear when it rains.

I didn't tell Cicero I was sorry. I didn't have a chance. But I'm not ready to rush up there and replay it the right way. What can I say? I can't believe how bad things have turned.

"Does God cry, Bub?"

"Jesus cried when his friend Lazarus died, and another time."

"When his mommy died?"

"No. His mommy was alive. He was looking at Jerusalem. The people in Jerusalem."

"Did he cry?"

"He did."

"Because they were bad?"

"Because they didn't know him. You didn't know that? I actually taught you something about the Bible? That's pretty good. You know, my mommy asks how you are in her letters. Have I ever told you that?"

"What's her name?"

"Monica. And she cries all the time."

"I was going to ask that."

"I know you were. I could see your little wheels turning. What's wrong? Don't be sad. What's the matter?"

The little guy falls straight down the well. It started with a furled lower lip and he was wet with tears in the space of a breath.

"Come on. It's okay to tell me what's wrong."

He keeps saying *'she'* but he can't finish. His breathing is all bollixed with wheezing.

"Who? Cissy? Yes? Aunt Cissy? She's just sad, sweetie. Come here. She's fine. It's a grown up thing. Breathe. Here. You have to stop crying. Listen, you want to hear a real secret? This is the real kind. But you have to stop crying. Okay? Your Aunt Cissy is going to have a baby, and God is making a home in her tummy where the baby can grow until it's ready to come out.
Sometimes when God makes the home in the tummy, mommies get grumpy. Did you know that's how babies get made?"

"Yes."

He's shaping up as fast as he fell apart.

"You're a smart boy. You have a good heart. Do you see anything in the rain?"

"Sort of."

"Do you really or not?"

"I don't want to say."

"Good. Maybe it's better not to talk for awhile."

I was wrong about my ear. Cicero *is* howling.

I was wrong about everything.

The punishment doesn't stop. This must be the part of the Program where the promises kick in. *Yeah*, the promises that say, 'We will not regret the past nor wish to shut the door on it,' and 'We will instinctively know how to handle situations that used to baffle us.' Surely I have arrived! Here I am, Lord; what's left of my trust is in you. How long will I suffer like this forever? I mean, I couldn't possibly be in a better position with Cicero. I'm no better than her pagan father. This must be what you meant in the garden, huh? When I foolishly thought myself in such high favor. The good life with my bad past!

"Bub?"

I've never told Marco that I don't like that name. It's from his mother's mouth. Right after he was born, Odessa thought I should be there with her instead of with Cicero. Impossible. And when it dawned on Odessa that we were through, she began to mock my sincerest overture with 'no thanks Bub.' I've never told Marco to bag the nickname, because I haven't decided what he should call me instead.

"Bub?"

"What."

"Do I have a daddy?"

"You know you do."

"I'm going to show you my daddy."

"I would like that."

"You're my daddy too."

"And you're my boy. There's no five-year-old in the world who I love more than you. Did you know that?"

"My daddy loves me, too."

"Yes he does. Yes he does."

Despair of Finding the Truth

My body is tense at rest. Rats in my elastic won't let me lie awake or fall asleep.

I'm trapped in this hall at the wall to the Boer side of the house. I can't crash downstairs and let Marco wonder why I'm not sleeping with Cicero. And I'm not going back into the bedroom to let Cicero saw me with her tongue.

I'll stay here as long as no one sees me.

I'm depending on Hack Man to be my wake up alarm, so that Cicero won't catch me here in the morning, shamed worse than my old man who crashed in the restaurant when my mom locked him out.

At least he slept on a carpet.

It's no good. I drift off for a time, but I'm brought back awake by the prod that this night is the lowest I ever got on my lowest day drunk.

The scary thing is that drinking doesn't seem like such a sad charade tonight.

This is worse than jail, because then I knew that getting out was a matter of time. It's worse than my Delta 88 crackup, because then Cicero cared. Worse than the Henry Hudson flip-over with Odessa, because then I was young and oblivious and feeling no pain.

The thing about tonight is that Cicero didn't mean we're finished. She meant we were finished fighting. But we're not finished fighting, because I haven't started. Call me unfit for fatherhood? There's only so much ammunition you can use against an attack like that around a five-year-old who has nothing to do but roam the three rooms of the house, playing the verbal version of connect-the-dots with the names of his mother, his uncle and his otherwise gentle Auntie Cis.

Now Cicero knows what it felt like for me to question my feelings for her after I found out about Stone. I had to rethink the times I thought we were happy, only to realize I was deceived. The fact is, if the dentist was my fault, then Odessa is Cicero's fault. It goes both ways or it doesn't go at all.

Cicero's lying to herself if she thinks she was always the one adjusting to me. I'm the one who gave up smoking and drinking and porno. What has she done beside change to a female gyno?

She said she never should have left Ann Arbor, but she didn't leave Ann Arbor because of me. She left because she had abandoned everything to Freud, and she was tired of being alone.

A fraud like Freud will never support you when the storm comes. I learned my lesson with Charlie Gul.

Instead of facing her facts, Cissy projects her empty nest on me. If anyone's unfit for parenthood, it's Cicero. She burdens me with her dad's infidelity and accuses me of my father's bad traits, and then throws the pregnancy in my face like I imposed it on her.

Okay. Wish you weren't pregnant? Wish it wasn't mine? Whose would you have it be, Stone's?

The problem is, when Cicero gets like this, you can't always believe her. I mean, I don't think Cicero would tell her mother about Odessa and me, and even if Cicero did, I can't imagine Emily Cruz telling Brutus. It would be bad psychology.

There are things Cissy has never told Emily Cruz, and I'm thinking this would be another one.

There must be twice as many things Emily Cruz has never told Brutus.

My legs are irate with agitation whether bent or straight, and my hips and shoulders are so sore that I can't find comfort in any position.

I know what I'll do. I'll lie on the bathroom floor and breathe in the shower steam. The mist has always taken me back to child time on the porch in St. Louis in the rain, and people with warm smiles and supportive voices whose relation I don't remember.

I creep downstairs, through the living room, where Marco is laid out in his little crucified pose on the hide-a-bed.

In the kitchen, the bass I grilled that no one ate is caught in the air.

I turn on the shower and fold Cicero's white pool towel for my pillow.

I haven't forgotten the back-stabber who threw me into this pan dance without my hands and feet.

I'll get Ori for this. Do no harm, huh? I'll *kill* him. I'll never talk to him again. A certain visceral satisfaction comes with the thought of avenging my crisis on him, and with the steam beading on my forehead, I feel a sensation of ease in my chest for the first time since Cissy called me off the mountain.

In the dark breath of early morning, between Hack Man coughs that pound nearby and birdcalls that seem to be circling me, I feel myself rising out of sunken sleep.

"I said *HEY*!"

Something surreal is happening in my half-sight. Cicero is barelegged in her open robe, shouting in harsh whispers and stepping out of the preposterous cutoff bloomers at her ankles.

"You told him!" She's out-of-her-mind angry, with spittle flying, and a frozen waffle broken in her fist.

Now I know what's going on. She's giving Marco his breakfast.

"You *DID*, didn't you!"

"Calm down."

"Don't you know how self-conscious he is! You know how insecure he is! I wanted you to get this solved with O.D.! Now I know why you didn't!"

"My mother sent me out into the world with nothing, girl."

"What are you talking about?"

"She gave me nothing to believe in. Told me my guess was as good as anybody's. Yeah, I told him. What was I going to do — what my mother did to me?"

"I don't know what you're talking about."

"Marco deserves the truth."

"What *truth* you son-of-a-bitch!"

"Your mouth wasn't bad enough last night?"

"Oh, right! Tell him I'm pregnant but don't tell him..." She mouths the words "*you're his father*" and swipes at me with a vulgar middle finger.

The gesture disgusts both of us equally, I think, so that the mist of the shower that had been our veil against a certain little witness now seems defiled.

Suddenly I think we each must have the same picture in our heads of innocent Marco, perched at the kitchen table, bracing for more violence to knife his tender sensibilities. Neither of us wants to go on with the escalation.

She's retreated inside herself where the coals never dim.

I want to tell her but I can't: "*Come on, girl! I'm already his father in everything but name.*"

For withholding what I should have said, I'm a coward.

I look like a mess in the mirror; a pressure rash the shape of a bitten apple on my cheek from the towel, and an eye stuck on a single night.

I don't know why I did it, girl: bedding Odessa. Stiffing you. Telling Marco about the baby. My latest stupid move. I do the same sober or drunk or saved.

I hear Cicero's school psychologist voice through the door, building up the little guy with all his happy options for waffle toppings and, by inference, his cheery life.

Kids don't need to know their options. They need to know their limits.

He can have molasses or powdered sugar. Lemon marmalade or Caro syrup. Or honey. He could try one dab on his plate first and then change his mind. "Or something else," she finally offers, which begs the question, especially for a kid: "What else is there?"

When I come out, they are both upstairs, mixing their quick steps and high speech in the hurry-purpose of distraction.

They're up to something without me. And a note on the table!

Wait a minute, it's a picture for me. Jesus with a small head and huge stick limbs on a cross, lined deep into the paper with pencil. Perhaps the long pencil streaks are rain, but I cannot be sure. Tears? Marco rushed it. Or he was rushed when Cicero saw it.

I sense Cissy's angry air as her heels click down the steps. When she comes around the corner she's dressed for the slums in a new tight white slit skirt, sunglasses, and her faded mustard-colored University of Michigan sweatshirt, ripped to show shoulder.

I mean to tell her to stop her little runway show. If she wants to play the look-at-what-I'll-leave-you-missing game, I can't stop her. But not with my Marco. I'm taking the boy to Mass.

"I'm walking him to church," I tell her.

"No." Her voice hides low in her throat. She's been crying. "I am."

"*You're* taking him to Mass?"

"I'm going to my mom's. Steuben will take him." She means Brutus. He's not a real man of faith.

"Wait a minute."

"There's no time."

I bend on my bad knees and hold out the picture to Marco that he made. I can see his eyes through her thighs. At first I thought Marco was hiding behind her legs but she's hiding him.

"This is great," I point to it. "I love pictures like this. Is this rain?"

"Bobby!" Cicero's exasperated.

I keep focus on Marco. He's my only chance.

"I want to tell you something." I'm not sure why this is choking me up. "I want to tell you that you don't have to show..." God, if I can't finish with a strong voice I'm going to lose everything. "You don't have to show me your father."

I want him to know I love him the way he is. I don't care about the tears. Just let me be clear without quivering!

"Marco..." His eyes drop down. I pick up their whites again, but my throat is not strong enough to bring anything out.

"Okay. Say bye-bye to your uncle." She's not letting me finish.

"Girl — " I rise up to put my hands on her if I have to but she shifts her watercolor eyes and leans away to get around me.

"I'll talk to you later." She turns her chin.

Nothing good has ever followed those words. So I tell her: "God spoke to me."

"Yeah?" She looks back incredulously, as though I'm having fun with her.

"He spoke to me, too." She strains with lips so retracted that I see the silver in her cavities. "I hope Steuben kicks your ass."

Here's a picture you never want to remember for the rest of your life: the backs of your wife and kid — a big hand tugging a little body forward, not *towards* the car but *away* from sadness.

You are the sadness, yet you wait for their smile as they roll away.

The painful taste of stretching space.

Fool. You are being left.

There is this thought pounding holes in your forehead: You are emasculated. Look casual in the door as if you don't know.

If you're honest with yourself about what she's doing, your only response as a man is to haul down the driveway after her and demand respect; to use a man's voice and a man's authority and command a new hearing by force.

But to stay here, framed like a six-inch pewter statue in the rearview mirror of Cicero's tampon-on-wheels, is to stand oblivious of the insult.

Which you must do.

You must, for the leaves on the driveway where the car has left.

Dead early.

Fallen from the Gingko tree. Leaves like stiff butterflies. And not yet Labor Day.

The brand of rejection is fire hot. The heart will not take it, man!

Hang every hope of escaping this on figuring out how the leaves turned and fell so early.

More leaves fall on Monday and Tuesday.

And Wednesday through Friday.

There is no decent answer why.

For any of it.

It strikes you what a happy companion pain is for loneliness.

There's no better mate!

Pain is the closest thing you have now. It knows you deeper than you do. It pushes you from behind into the hard night, and calls you out where you don't want to go into another morning of harsh light.

Pain tells you why you shouldn't eat and why you can't sleep. It becomes indispensable counsel in that way, so that you can't throw it out, even when it fouls all your hope to reconcile.

Then look what happens. Pain takes a friend named revenge.

They frolic in plans all day long to settle sore scores with Cicero and Origen.

Nothing gives more pleasure in sterile times.

AA calls that resentment. And resentment kills more drunks than anything else. But I don't call that resentment. I call that contentment.

Sport for the brain!

I took Cicero from a big black bag to little white tops, and Origen from Count No-Count to AA Sage First-Class.

They're both headed where the smoke never stops because they failed to acknowledge the coming of their Lord.

I'm serious.

This Pontiac Parisienne sounds like it's on the last revolution every time I take it out now. It jitters so bad in idle that I have to shift into neutral and gun the gas to keep it from knocking out.

But once I get it onto the highway to Dickens, it will run.

It will have to.

I told Flaco before he died that I would get his suitcase. It's taken me a year to do it, but I'm keeping my word.

I need a mission.

I can't watch the horizon all alone on High Street another night longer.

Flaco's suitcase has some dope in it and a suicide note, supposedly, with good lines that cracked me up. But when I told him I didn't exactly believe the part about the note and wanted to see it myself, he got angry.

Sometimes the guy lied.

He was funny as hell; I just didn't like him telling me certain things were true when I knew they weren't. He had this great story about a Park Avenue stitch queen who used to give him change from her fur and every once in a while an earring or a Franc was in it, until one night he stopped her with the really good rap, "Gimme something love has touched to last me a little longer." Made the woman bawl.

Only trouble was he lied.

He never spoke so pretty to someone so petty, and certainly not on cue. But I overlooked it. Flaco was a true friend.

Pete the Breeze is the closest thing I have left to life out there.

So this is how I spend my Saturday. Sitting here at the junction of The Short Road to Hell and Life on God's Terms, revving at the red light and watching the girl in the meadow across the street flush in the face, trying to pull down the boy with the ball.

It's a pickup football game. She fills out a flower power dress like a college senior, but there's enough kid in her to still want this tackle *bad*. The boy's her own size, but he won't come down. She has clamped one hand on each of his shoulders, yanking on him with her knees bent and off the ground, and her bare feet flailing above the grass. She won't tackle him because she doesn't have the mass.

Someone should tell her the only way to beat him is to let go of him.

Dickens is where Flaco lived. It's one of those places where you can crack a yawn at the border and hit the hamlet line at the train tracks before your mouth is closed. The houses are built right up onto the road.

No one walks out. No one goes in.

The industry here is of two kinds — hauling wrecks and junkyarding wrecks. All you see is gravel and vines because there's motor oil under every surface. The raccoons pull the chicken bones out of the garbage and leave the diapers on the road. It's the kind of place where the Rebel Flag is on the bedroom headboard, and girls pose for Polaroids with open legs.

I don't feel like explaining how I know that.

It's best to think about something else when you're in Dickens, like how you ended up here, sitting at the tracks in a Parisienne while your boy is being turned against you by a cock major and a soft-peddling New Age shrink who have planted every bad seed in Cicero's mind about you.

The answer is worse than the question; there's no fun in the irony. Coming here was the best idea you've had all week.

Ask yourself why you should go on.

You can't go to AA to see Pete the Breeze because Origen is looking for you, and you can't get pumped up about drinking this one out, because what do you do for an encore? Start the program over? Pretend you aren't an alcoholic? Fake your big questions like the answers don't matter?

You can't drink because you don't believe in it anymore.

And you can't pray because you see nothing in faith. You knelt at your bed and now you sleep alone. You asked God to protect you, and Brutus and his recruits wait at the gate to tear you up. For what! For being presumptuous! For thinking it could all change! For believing the Gospel and the Program promises instead of Origen and Seagull? Why, for crying out loud! For wanting to protect Cicero!

Fine. It's no use. Let the girl go. I got news for you, girl. If I can't change, then neither can you. Go to Stone. Go ahead, do it. Roll right up to

the train tracks. Phyllis Stein is going to fire you because you can't point
to the last good thing you did for her. You write stories before you figure them out. You don't care about the questions you ask, so you don't question the answers you get. Your deceit has no end. You think you know truths because you read them in the Bible and the AA Big Book, and you think that saying them is the same as doing them. You think that admiring them is the same as following them.

Welcome to the hell of your own doing.

The only way you'll see Marco is if you take him, and you aren't going to do that.

Look at you.

You can't even compare yourself better than your last mistake.

You have no momentum.

Go ahead and run back to where the cups were good. It won't work, because that's where Charlie Gul is, and the fact that you can't face is worse than all of this together: you haven't armed yourself with a single weapon against Seagull this whole year sober. You're stripped weaker than when you left him. What are you going to do about his $70,000?

What are you waiting for? Why don't you just go? Gas the self-examined life and the shrieking horn and the white light.

The train is a brown monster of blurring speed, coming from the left in a surreal instant of dust glitter and dizzy light, with the odor of hot, filthy oil, and the certainty that when I close my eyes I'll be crushed to all hell.

I'm shot lunging the instant after the God-awful hollow smash and stinking metallic echo hits the left front of the Parisienne, forcing choking burned-rubber smoke into my nose and numbing, wet sensations through my arm and legs.

God, I'm going to drink my own death!

I'm pierced with train shrieks, and vibrating with my neck still wrenched back as the car skids bumping across the embankment against the wheel angles.

It slows its slide into the second back yard.

The black guts of the car engine spit orange-white sparks, and I hurl forward with a sudden stomach heave that stops halfway up my chest with acid burning. My face pricks with sweat, and the pain is like fire in my arm. Oh God, my hand! I feel it but I don't see it!

The car still jerks skidding sideways, but the faintness in my head passes.

Cranberries are all over my windshield.

My left arm is attached here where it belongs. It feels like a knife is gutting my forearm from the wrist to the elbow, but it's here. I didn't know where it was for a second.

The car comes to rest in coarse gravel.

Something else is wrong.

My right leg is wet.

Oh Christ. What's *that* on my leg?

I'm just breathing and thinking now.

The sulfur rubber chemical stench with the warm blood in my throat is bearable if this is as bad as it gets. Looking up track, the red train lights aren't moving. The train must be stopped. Behind me in the rear view mirror, there's no one in the house, but the black dog on the rope is up, stiff with stupid beast worry.

The driver's side and hood panels were sheared off the car. The windshield cranberries are my forearm and knuckle skin, caught in the spider web of cracked glass. I pissed on myself, but it's oddly comforting and warm, like soup. I can move my toes. I even turned the ignition off with my left hand and took out the keys.

Ha! I turned the ignition off, damn it!

I keep thinking if I sit here long enough I'll figure out what I'm not comprehending. Something past me. But each moment something new hurts, and I can't concentrate. Now it's my neck. Maybe if I pull the glass out of my forearm it will stop throbbing and feel less like fire.

It was a Conrail.

A 3:19 Conrail.

I had my tires on the track. It's coming back to me. I had driven around the cross buck and butted my tires right up on the rail. But I'm still here. I perched the Parisienne in front of a freight train and I'm still alive. *You are sadness, and sadness cannot leave sadness.*

The caboose lights up track haven't moved. The driver thinks I'm dead.

He doesn't know what to do next.

I do. I'm not staying to play 20 questions with the cops so I can spend another month in the hospital. I'm getting out.

It's heartening to put weight on my feet and feel my bones walk away from the Parisienne, and when I curl my forearm in a sling position, the throbbing isn't so fierce.

The strides across the gravel kick my brain out of stop-shock. Move a muscle, change a thought — an AA coupon that actually works when you need it.

The more I get away from the car, the more I realize that I should keep moving. Not that Dickens is the kind of place where anyone would notice a skinned Parisienne in the backyard, or a bleeding punk with piss down his leg walking on the shoulder.

The motion of going *some*where is the closest thing to relief I've felt all week.

It doesn't last.

I don't feel lighter for escaping the train, or any heavier for losing my car. I feel hollow in both directions, down to the darkest level. There is nobody in my life after 27 years who has been strong enough to stay with me, and nothing so calamitous in life to take me out of the game all together.

I'm here, and I can't help it or hurt it enough.

I know what: I'll go to the city. I'll go to the Porticoes. Sure! I should've thought of it sooner, although the idea of going down there dopeless sober without so much as a lousy cigarette to roll is less tempting than the thought's first rush.

I have to admit, I knew that Flaco's suitcase was a dead mission for the same reason. Who would keep his suitcase anyway?

I wish I had the Parisienne just to get me to High Street. I'd run it off the ridge!

It was finished with me before I was finished with it.

What little I had left is gone.

When I pick the blood crusts off my forearm, it opens more bleeding, but I do it anyway because the clots have glass grains in them.

My wrist broke the windshield, but I didn't break my wrist.

I see it all again. Slow motion brown whir. White light freeze frame. The putrid petrol odor and blasting smash. A metal coat pealed clean to the ripped-up chops underneath.

I never saw the Jeep rollover with Odessa coming, and I never felt it after it was over.

One more pound of pressure from the roll bar against Odessa's neck, and she would have been paralyzed. Or snapped dead.

Her face was pinned on the pavement. The road had torn open a new mouth. It was a ghoulish mandible, and her hair was stuck in the distress as I hung there, upside down in the shoulder harness, coughing and sweating and looking at the red teeth in her open jaw.

It wasn't a horror because I didn't feel a thing. Nothing was real when I was drinking. Not the arrest on possession or the pregnancy test or my eye patch.

And now I know what I couldn't figure out in the Parisienne at the tracks. I was looking right at it. It was my prosthesis. Pupil-side up on the passenger's seat floor. The stone-sterile stare of a dead fish eye. I couldn't figure out what it was because it wasn't mine.

Nothing looks so false and faithless as a fake eye out of socket. *Leave it there!* Don't go back for it. Why retrieve that untrue thing? And why pretend, after all this, that it makes any difference what I do or how I think or who I believe? Origen is right. There's no changing who you are, unless you get hit with a white light. And you don't get hit with a white light, because you're one of the dregs.

Your naive hope that God will pity your desperation is like playing poker with no chips. No chips, no game. No game, no act! Which fits fine. Act or no act.

Nobody's buying it anyway.

"Bah-bee!" It's a fat voice from the past.

I spin around and see that I'm right. Across the parking lot of 1-2-3 Deli. It's Tony Trapdoor.

No matter what you do, he always falls through.

"Bah-bee!" The guy was in the Program for a while but he didn't last. He's a sentimental crowd-pleaser and a decent-hearted oaf, but he lies to himself and he'll never make it outside of the rooms.

He slams his trunk shut on two bags of ice.

"Bah-bee, bay-bee. How ya doing? You still in da rooms?"

"I'm still an alcoholic." You enormous white fraud. Look at him wedge that mound of back fat into his toy-size Camaro. He must weigh two-fifty.

"You, I always listened to Bah-bee. You know? You told the trute."

"You never listened to anybody, did ya big guy?"

"Heh. No. But you, I liked you."

He's not even looking at me.

I've got blood on my shirt, a urine roll down my leg, a rotten eyeball, and I'm still spitting red. I thought earlier I had merely bit my tongue, but now it feels like a deep cut back there. What the hell do you do with a cut in your tongue like that?

"You look good Bah-bee. Maybe I'll see you one night. Surprise!"

"We're doing new math in the rooms."

"Yeah? *New* huh?" At that he twists the key and his Camaro snarls.

"One in ten is a drunk."

"That ain't new Bah-bee. Funny guy!"

"Ten percent find recovery, the other ninety percent get sober when they die."

"You crack me in half."

"One outta three in recovery makes it. One outta three."

"Hey, I called my sponsor last week. I tol' him I'm gonna come around but I been so busy, as the facts go."

"One outta three."

"That's the *new* math, huh Bah-bee!"

"There's a meeting tonight."

"I'm gonna come around maybe. Some of dem people I don't love. But you, Bah-bee. Gimme somethin.' Always the trute."

His huge hand is hanging wide of the window for skin, but I don't give the Trapdoor anything.

He's got two cases of Coors in his back seat. And he laughs as his Camaro howls up the highway.

The walk is not good on my bad knees. There was a point when my sponsor Jared of the Sorrows had me convinced that I should be *thankful* for having knees that work at all after breaking them both in the Delta 88.

The fact is, the same God that gave me good knees was the one watching over me when I lost the brake and hit the wall. The same God that saw to it that I had four good months at Burke rehab is the one who brought me to Dickens to drink death for a third time.

Once upon a time my knees were euphemisms for my new walk, but now they act just like the Parisienne: one day they'll fail too. Each step I take on them is like a mile deeper into the unknown country, so that the walk to the garden a week ago on the holy mountain seems like it never happened.

There's nobody on the platform when I get to the train station.

The tin sepulchers that run from here to Manhattan are only filled on weekdays.

And God forbid that a provider should run into an embarrassment like me on the launch pad.

Isn't that right!

Cicero thinks I'm a lousy provider. I've been telling her men protect, God provides.

My, is *that* stupid.

Makes me wonder why I even go on.

I'm not going to ask why anymore. The question is too weak! It never gets a serious answer.

Now I see why Ori can't reconcile the book of Job. Suddenly neither can I. So Job loses everything and his friends condemn him instead of console him. Fine. So God works in mysterious ways. Fine.

But that's not the burden of the book. The burden of the book is that God gives Job over to the devil, and when Job wants to know why, God gives him the bollocks. The fingers under the chin. The mountain goat squatting with kid!

Guess what, Lord? I know your ways are higher than my ways. That's the whole point. I have a new question. It's called what *now*! The Program would call that projection, but not me! I call that *protection*. I want to know what's next!

And here's the answer. Coming down the track, only this time from the right. And it ain't the 3:19. This time it's the 6:53. And again I remember the cross buck in the moment of the white frozen light. In one second I could've inched forward and it would have been over.

For good.

Suspended in Doubt

It's one of those late September nights just after the rain where the street is glossed as black as licorice. The moisture conducts echoes through the air in a compound clamor, so the laughing and music seem to come from a car under teenage influence, but you can't find it, and the shrill sound of white women with wine coming from Paco del Norte one block up seems like it shouldn't be so sharp on your ear as it is.

Ordinarily, I don't walk this way through town, because I take the shortcuts, but tonight I need the extra territory to walk off my worry.

I'm going back to my home AA group to suffer the backlash from Jared of the Sorrows for staying away without calling him for three weeks.

It doesn't pay to go around to other AA groups, no matter how often I explain my mess in strange rooms; they can't help me because they don't know me.

The Paco's women are white — I was right — but they're drinking Margaritas instead of wine. The one with the short brown bouffant wears a camisole the color of new pennies that pulls up on her back, showing the knots of her spine before it dives under the waist of her tan Spandex leggings. Her friends wear the white T-shirt tops with high-cut sleeves, and they tuck their calves under the wire mesh chairs.

The bouffant with the copper top dangles a clog sandal on the bend of her big toe, so that I follow the line of her almond-skinned shin to the thick crease of her crossed thigh, committing me to look at her. But the bouffant is not looking at me. She is looking at my patch.

I cut the patch from Cicero's brown leather bra cup. It looks *fine.* I could confront the bouffant right here on the street and ask her what the hell she's looking at. But I save it. She's just a chick with tequila who doesn't matter.

Cicero would have said something to me if the patch looked so bad.

Come to think of it, I can't be sure how closely Cicero was paying attention to me.

She wanted to meet me in the hallway after Marco's Kindergarten open house. She kept me waiting until I was the last parent left. And I got stuck talking to a nun who knows Odessa.

Cicero had called me at High Street a couple of days after Dickens, because the cops traced the Parisienne to her. And she said Marco wanted me to come to parents' night. Fine, I said. I didn't mention on the phone that I knew Cissy had come back to the house while I was at work to get clothes and her bleach-green hat.

And I didn't ask about the poem that I found when I was looking through every scribble of her stuff, or the six Latin words in a frame that was in her drawer, or when she thought we should talk, or what exactly she wanted from me now.

I just said 'okay.'

And I showed up at the open house.

Marco asked every question three ways about the patch but Cicero didn't say anything. She stayed on the rim of the conversation with her legs together, her hands folded atop her purse, and her belly bowled beneath a ribbed red sweater. My child.

I didn't say anything to her either. Except to ask how she felt. Cicero said "Fine," and "Still in AA?"

That's what got me back into the rooms. I figured if AA was the one thing she asked about, it was the one thing that still had her interest.

But no, I didn't go straight back to my home group at St. Francis Church, because it has been a full time job avoiding Origen in Mount Kisco and at the newsroom and at my own house, where he had never dared to come before.

I wound up hitting AA meetings in Yonkers and White Plains and Peekskill. They gave me a purpose each night, but I kept thinking about Tony Trapdoor, crying uncontrollably through a case of Coors, showing up at St. Francis, and not seeing me there to encourage him with the trute. I scared myself with the thought of Tony shooting all the dogs.

The Trapdoor owns a boarding kennel.

The shrill yappings of the white tequila women play deep in the distance as the street grows darker at the edge of downtown, and I take shorter steps, waiting for the wall of St. Francis to appear around the corner.

It's more than the Trapdoor.

I can't figure what 'Give Up Your Picture' means. I thought at first the 'picture' was the dream restaurant centerfolds in my Chef Today magazines. So I threw out six years' worth of them. I thought the regret I felt after tossing them was sorrow for the loss of those dear things, until it hit me a day later that I didn't want them back.

I wanted to give up my picture, whatever that meant, and I still hadn't done it.

Then I thought it must be my old girlfriend photographs from high school in St. Louis and my one year at DePaul in Chicago. I threw out the box after I looked at them. Next I grabbed my punk rock tapes from the days on Avenue A when Cissy and I would mail letters with upside down stamps, and I dropped those in a bag that's gone for good. I kept the Violent Femmes tapes since the Femmes converted to Gospel songs, and I kept the Psychedelic Furs, because I can't conclude from the lyrics anything irreverent about "Heaven" or "Imitation of Christ."

After I did it, I didn't have anything left to bag, so I looked out the window across the street and watched the horses eat grass at Bel Farm, wondering why I still felt adrift of the anchor.

It was because I hadn't done anything yet.

Then it struck me about the frogs.

Jared many months back told me a Native American parable about three frogs that I didn't understand. The first part went: 'three frogs sitting on a log make a decision to jump in the water. How many are left?' The answer is three: They only *decided* to jump.

The second part went: 'three frogs sitting on a log make a decision to jump in the water. Two jump, the other turns blue.'

You are never the same once you make a decision.

As I watched the horses, I started to take encouragement.

I was different, but I still needed to act.

And from there the thought crept up that God's finger must be on my recipes.

In four thick ring binders. I was going to make a book out of them. God! Those? I expelled the thought and tried an end-around that night by searing foi gras with tournedos and béarnaise.

I burned the fat right on the flame and smoked it like an Old Testament offering, but it was no good. The meat was not edible and I still felt the weight of God's finger on me. Next morning I threw the recipes out. The pages were full of booze. I didn't have the patience to rip out every recipe that called for Tio Pepe or Cointreau or Pear Williams.

It all had to go.

I knew I was still off target when I didn't feel lighter in heart by that night, but worse.

I threw out what was never mine.

It isn't the recipes or the pictures or the punk or the magazines. Whatever it is I'm supposed to give up I still have.

That's a hell of a thing to say about someone who has nothing left.

We inhabit our own world of unmentionable fears and childish hopes and shameful regrets and top secret dreams that no one can share no matter how near to our hearts they are.

We enter our world alone. And we inhabit it alone. People search the world around them, but not the world inside them. The world inside is the only unexplored territory worth the risk of discovery. And in that respect, I do have something left. If I can't run a masterpiece restaurant or save runaways, then I need to figure out who I am: it's the only mission I can actually execute.

St. Francis' high wall of fieldstones is striated with flood lights, and I realize that I am doing the right thing by coming back here. I have faith that inside those walls I'm going to get an answer. The uncanny thing about AA is there is always an angel in the rooms. It might be a newcomer 10 days sober or an old timer crotch like Frighthairs. You never know who's going to tell you exactly what you need to hear. Sometimes you need to hear it come out of your own mouth.

Inside the church, I hear laughing in the basement. The meeting has already started and I'm late. I'm late because of my half steps the last block to church, late because I didn't take the short cut, late because I always wait too long to get anywhere on time.

I set myself up in the back, opposite a cracked beveled mirror, so that I can play the sight angles without people knowing my eye's on them. It is an older crowd tonight – 80 people or more –

and I don't see Pete the Breeze or any of the Friday night boys.

Leading the meeting is Audrey the Irrelevant, who dropped her baby on his head 25 years ago and still talks about it when she shares like it's frightfully potent. It isn't.

They're laughing because Grady the Swearing Gearhead is sharing something gritty. Something vulgar from the fingernails of his greasy world. Everyone thinks Grady the Swearing Gearhead is a riot. He curses at all the right clauses and says "You know," incessantly when he's making no connection in the world except that toilet humor still gets nervous laughs.

For some reason he stopped being funny just now, and the clicking of my quarter heels on the cement floor as I pace has become the main punctuation in the place.

The guy in front of me frowns. It's Lone Male Claude: thin, retentive, tremor-prone. I get no 'how-ya-doing' glance from Lone Male Claude. That's a cold brush, Claude. It's because I'm late and I've been away from this room for three weeks. No. It's because of my patch. What's the matter, Claude, you jealous? I know. This is the closest you've gotten to a bra since you were weaned.

I don't feel syrupy-sweet towards Claude.

Fact is, you don't have to like everyone in the Program, and you can dump on anyone in the rooms as long as you do it the AA way. You have to qualify your share with "For me." and you have to keep the focus on yourself, without naming names. Then you can damn your own mother. It's a pronoun game, and it's harder to pull off than it sounds.

"Bobby?"

What's The Irrelevant doing calling on me when my hand isn't up? That's only pulled on newcomers.

People always bust protocol on me in the rooms.

"You decided to join us, Bobby. You want to check in?"

"My name is Bobby and I'm an alcoholic."

"Hi, Bobby."

"Date of my last drink is August fourth of last year, this is my group and I stayed sober today by hitting my knees, keeping it simple, and getting to this meeting."

Suddenly I'm self-conscious — not about what I'm going to share, but about where Ori is. I don't see him but I know he's here. I tense up thinking he is going to skewer me as soon as I'm finished.

I can't decide how to bullet-proof my share. Now I've delayed too long. I have to say something.

"I know I haven't been showing up, but I've been going around other meetings, and I'm doing what I need to do to stay sober." I'm looking at the floor, but it's okay. The acoustics in here are remarkable. And my voice carries. So I go for it: the big share.

"I was at a prayer retreat last month and I heard this voice in my heart say 'Give up your picture' and I thought I had it figured out. I mean, I thought I knew what I was supposed to do. It isn't like I hear voices. I don't hear voices. But I did hear 'Give up your picture' in my heart and I was sure it meant this dream I've had forever to own my own restaurant and how that's the wrong dream to have now because I can't have the booze around obviously. So I got rid of my chef magazines. But that wasn't it. Then I threw out the pictures and the old love letters and the tapes I listened to in college and I still had a heavy heart about the whole thing. So I got drastic and tossed these recipes I had from a joint my old man ran into the ground in Chicago. I still don't know what the picture is. All I know is what the picture isn't. The picture isn't in magazines or memories or music. And it isn't my spices either."

Someone laughs. It's a Vietnam vet who never takes off his POW hat. He thinks I'm a joke. Maybe I am. But I have the floor.

"The picture has nothing to do with them. It's me. Something I'm holding. Something I can't figure out because I can't see it. I have to keep praying and coming to meetings."

Jared of the Sorrows has his hand up. Five other hands shoot up, too. They all want a crack at me. Jared of the Sorrows will get called on, even though he's despised, because he's my sponsor and he'll let me have it worse than anyone else. Old timers love to see someone like me get ironed.

"Hi my name is Jared and I'm an alcoholic"

"Hi Jared."

Jared got sober 21 years ago when he was 19. One night, 13 cognacs, three dead friends in a car and that was it for Jared. When he gives his sobriety date people who don't know him think he's a god until he starts to share.

He misuses his tremendous advantage of heavyweight sober time to enforce AA orthodoxy, to hammer heresy, and to pontificate past the point of charity, so that people constantly show Jared their backs for his 'honesty.'

"No one tells a pigeon that this journey will be easy or pain free," Jared says, tossing back the loopy hair curls from his eyes in a contemptible upturned no-no shake — a habit I hate more than him calling me a pigeon. "What we say is that you don't have to do it alone. Why do we say that? Let's look at it."

Yeah, Jared. Let's look.

"This is a disease of isolation that wants you to believe you're unique. But we say no, our problem is not unique. We have a common solution. That's why this is a 'we' program, not a 'me' program."

Wanker.

"Our common solution says it's not enough to recognize that we have a problem beyond our control and that we need to reach for God's help with all the desperation of a drowning man for a life preserver. It demands action. We are dealing with a mind that doesn't want to follow directions. I want the medicine but I won't follow the prescription."

He's patting his chest as though he means himself.

"I want to design my own recovery program because I'm unique. And I know that if I call my sponsor, he'll tell me that I'm not unique, that I'm a green drunk with the same old war stories, and that these steps are numbered because we take them in order, as a requirement for recovery. What kind of mind wants what it can't have before its time? What is time? Time is 'things I must endure,' 'things I must earn.' What kind of a mind thinks it can beat time? A mind of fear. Fear wants to 'fuck everything and run.' But we say no, fear must 'face everything and recover.'"

I stopped listening to Jared because I got tired of counting the coupons.

He's moving on anyway to share about some inane inadequacy in his own life, because he is a profoundly lonely man. Even he realizes that he ought to have more fruit to show for his astonishing record of sobriety. Such as a girlfriend.

I know that Jared didn't want me to go on the prayer retreat, because I didn't have my 12 steps, but what was I going to do? I've already been through this a thousand times. I was *trapped.*

A voice snaps me back to attention. It's the under water words of Ori. He's here.

"What we're looking at tonight *is* unique, because when you cut the myth away from the man you put him in enemy territory," Ori says. "When you go in alone like the kid here, no one wants to recognize what you're trying to do, so you have to become an inventor or a martyr. Either way you can't re-enter the camp until the priest says you're clean."

I see a partial profile of Ori's enormous forehead, two rows in, by the far wall. But something is different about him.

Something is bizarre about this whole night.

It's more than the fact that Audrey the Irrelevant has called on the two most despised AA old timers in northern Westchester, who are both talking about me.

It's beyond me.

"We know the kid did the wandering in the wasteland deal, but he dropped his little bread crumb trail and found his way back."

Ori is different. What is it?

"To the extent that he can crack the oracle or be the new man when no one is watching is another deal, but if this is his homecoming party the road outside looks better, so let's cut him a break and call off the Program police."

I still don't see Origen in full, and I don't want to be any more conspicuous by moving to my left for a better view.

A growing part of me appreciates what Ori is doing, but most of me wants to run him through, thinking how hypocritical he is to support me now, after all the damage he's done by calling Cicero.

The chair-scooting and key jingling and clock-checking begins too early for me tonight. I would have liked the meeting to go until midnight. I don't mind people giving me their two cents about my 'picture,' because the more you live with unanswered questions, the less appealing your own thinking becomes.

At the same time, I'm in no mood to get my latest act reviewed.

The Irrelevant closes the meeting, and as we stand to say The Lord's Prayer, I resolve to get out before Ori or Jared can harangue me.

But when we finish I turn to see Charlotte's Web in my path, grinning her wide mouth at me. The first and second things that jump into my head are 'You ruined my escape.' and 'Men with the men, women with the women.'

"I did what you said," she says. Charlotte is fat, but she's an expert dresser with the long skirts and mid-calf boots and undone button blouses, so that you don't stay interested imagining how fat she really is. Her maroon finger nails are lined up in a grip on a ceiling pole. She also hasn't meddled any about my patch, although she's locked in on it twice.

Something about her posture holds me here when I should know better and bolt.

"I did what you said," she says again.

"With the garlic, you mean?" I ask. Her breasts spill forward. Am I'm supposed to believe that they could fall out at any moment? She must have practiced this pole dance at home.

"It wilted like you said." She didn't hear me. She's not the only one thinking about something else. She means the leaf spinach. I gave her a greens recipe. I don't believe she ever used it. This is a bread and butter girl. Her breasts are as fat as thighs.

Jared closes in with cowboy boots and waves Charlotte away using the back of his hand.

Origen strides up from my blind side in the same instant, with his scalp shaved clean and pink.

Mercy! I've never seen a head so bare-enormous! This is Origen Alexander's prelude to the bridge.

"Where have you been?" Jared asks me.

"Busy at work," I tell him.

I can't believe Origen is a skin head.

"What about you, Jared?" Ori says. "Anywhere interesting?"

"I was in Ohio for the convention. We drove to Akron where they had the first group in the back of Dr. Bob's office."

"Did you see the proctoscope?" Ori acts more interested in the chocolate cup cake he took off the table than his own question.

The act doesn't fool anyone. He has a scarlet cluster of cuts on the crest of his skull that look as fresh as sweat.

"What did you say?" Jared of the Sorrows asks. Origen looks at him and loads the entire cake into his mouth."

"Well I guess we won't find out now," says Jared, winking at me.

"Ori chews unharassed.

"You said something," Jared tells him.

"Do you know what a proctoscope is?" Ori asks.

Jared does his upturned no-no shake.

"To examine the anus," Ori says. "Dr. Bob was a proctologist."

Jared straightens: "Well, this *is* a program of assholes. Ha ha ha!"

And with that, Jared of the Sorrows showed us *his* back.

"See that?" Origen says. "We each had our say, but in a sober way."

"And now I'll have mine." I walk past him, but in the wrong direction without thinking. My only exit is up the stairs that go behind the altar.

"Hey, Byline — " he gets a hold of my wrist and that sets me off.

"WHAT! You told her, didn't you!"

"Wrong question, Byline."

"Games!"

"Whoa, Erasmus."

"More games!"

"In the land of the blind, the one-eyed man is king."

"What are you talking about?"

"You, Byline."

"Never again, you hear!" I take my escape the same way I started, up the dark stone steps of the back stairwell.

"Where are you going? You can't get out that way, Byline! Hey, Dante! I'm on your side."

"My side, huh?" I see in the dark a red blade of light beamed across the threshold. "What side is that?"

"Will you slow down? It's like the Labyrinth in here. Want to split hairs, Byline, okay. The truth is colossal. You have to side with it, even when the truth goes against you."

"So you told Cicero!"

"I didn't tell Cicero anything, Byline. What would I tell her that she doesn't already know?"

There is an eerie sway to his words, something that registers worthiness in my ears, although distant.

I would like to believe Ori. But I can't be fooled anymore. I want to see proof before I trust him again.

I push into the sanctuary and see that the light under the door was coming from a lone altar candle hanging in a blood-colored glass from a braided chain. I may as well be hypnotized by the thing. I have no more urge to head down the aisle to check if those huge double doors are open than I do to look for a hiding place up in the choir loft. My escape plan seems ridiculous now.

There is a high calm in the empty church, and a feeling of even breathing very near. It's the same presence I felt among the faces of favor in the garden.

"Sorry, Byline. I was delayed by the Minotaur."

His nicked scalp is hideous in the sanctuary shadows, and the dark ovals of his wire-rim glasses are as black as the cavities of an empty skull.

"Byline. The Minotaur."

He wants credit for the quip.

"The monster," I mouth dully.

"The metaphor."

"Who do you think you are, always peddling parables?"

"Out of the frying pan and into the fire, Byline. Is that better? Is that *pedestrian* enough for you? I know you think I did something, and what happened at home with Penelope will change if you get the blame right, but I got to be honest with you — you came to the mountain with the big question and you went downhill with your own answer. We talked about doing no harm, but you're hummin' Gypsy songs if you think your only care was sparing Cicero pain. The only spare deal you cared about was your own."

"You could say that about anyone."

"Yes I could. And yet I haven't. I have said it about someone. And someone has to tell you, Byline, you can't be the new man to avoid the old man."

I look at him incredulously. That's the only expression I have for a preposterous comment like that.

Yet in my chest where I am on guard and still sore there comes a releasing that feels like a melting. It rends what Origen just said easier to accommodate.

I can't say why.

"Says who?" I must seem sad, because he looks concerned.

"You may not have the truth, Byline, but you're far from error."

"I mean what you just said before."

"I know what I said, Byline. And so do you."

The melting is like a thawing, a warming, but without a temperature change. A wonderful thing.

There is an iron latticework gate behind the altar with an open arched entranceway. Behind it is the hanging candle with the rose-yellow flame.

The dissolving in my chest brings a lightening. Not a lightening of weight, but a brightening of darkness. The darkness actually takes a shape in the surrounding light. A shade of understanding. And the understanding rises to the surface.

It was always about getting away for me. It was never about committing anew.

I repented, I turned away. But I never looked at what I was turned towards with the same fervor as what I was turned against.

"So you're saying I'm not sincere."

"Sincerity is a verbal fig leaf, Byline. It hides our shame. It means without wax, not without cracks. The ancients used to plug the marble idols with wax, but the righteous merchants sold their gear sin *cere*. Without wax. No, Byline, I'm not accusing you of insincerity. I'm accusing you of more ambition than that."

This is what Origen calls being on my side? Now I *am* leaving him.

"No more rabbit holes, Dante. I'm not chasing you down anymore. You want to sit here and listen to what I have to say, I'll tell you exactly what I mean. Nice patch by the way, what is that, a décolleté?"

"What did you use on your head, a paring knife?"

"Ah, Byline. A peasant like me with cutlery?"

I must look in bad shape, because he is coming over to the confessional, where I'm gripped with the thought that I did a lot of suffering the last three weeks staying away from him.

"Byline? You can't appreciate the irony? Can you see me with a paring knife?"

"You would have killed yourself with it a long time ago."

"Is that nice?"

"That's the point."

"No, it's a total non sequitur. That's the point. Look at me. God doesn't love us with a love of attraction, Byline. He loves us with a love of creation. He delights in the hidden things that he put there in you. That's how he can love you when you know he should loathe you. Now that is good and bad. The good part is you'll never find love like that on earth. The bad part is you'll never find love like that on earth."

"How can you say that?"

"Even I have my moments."

"After everything you said about the short arm of God and the allegory of the Gospels. What about your Agency and Empathy!"

"You gotta stop damning the infidels, Byline."

When Ori says 'agency' he means God, and when he says 'empathy' he means love — but human love, unaided from above.

And every time Ori tells me there is no God without human love it's like another tick on the Bulletin of Atomic Scientists' clock. I feel like if I don't disarm this bad formula before Ori says "Time's Up! I'm blowing my head off," then I'll hang the remedy for the human condition and blow *my* head off. So I tell him: "I'm talking about you."

"So am I. You gotta drop this fundamental illness with the Bible thumping crowd that damns the only creature that's saved. That's the artist's job."

"That's God's job."

"I hate to break your heart, but Hamlet had more impact on Western civilization than John's Gospel."

"How can you say that?"

"Without art, the truth would kill you."

"The truth doesn't kill you. The truth sets you free."

"The truth doesn't set you free. The truth convicts you. Come on, Byline! Where's your sense of self-deprecation? If God is so systematic about who he saves and who he smites, how come he saved Odessa first?"

What did that heretic just say?

"Tell me anything, Byline. Tell me you're weighing a rejoinder. Tell me you're deliberating between two tacts. Or finding the right verse to mangle. Read me the label inside that fucking brassiere. Say anything except you don't have an answer. If you can pick out the lost from the saved by the attendance sheet in church on Sunday, why did God save that little tart Odessa before you?"

I have no idea why.

"You have no idea why. It's because she's more useful to him than you. Where are you going?"

Somebody tell that heretic I don't have to answer where I'm going.

"There's no devil stoking the hell fire, Byline! And there's no praying to God for his will. We *have* his will. It's called love each other as I have loved you. Get it? Stay away from the God squad that damns infidels. Nobody wants to follow a church like that because there is a little principle called yank the plank from you own eye before you dust the speck out of mine, but that doesn't register with your ilk when you come crusading with your theological coupons, does it?"

He's talking about my church. We're evangelicals, not fundamentalists. He knows that, but he won't respect the distinction because he feels threatened. Well guess what? So does everyone.

I'm getting out of here, back the way I came. Down the steps that are darker than the Porticoes after three.

"Listen, Byline. I heard what you were trying to say in the meeting but like I tried to explain, no one is going to cheer for that."

"I didn't say it for claps, for God's sake."

"Didn't say you did. Why do I always have to chase you off-stage?"

"Maybe I really *do* want to give up my picture."

"Maybe you want to see what it is first."

"Be Jonah if I don't like it?"

"If it's from God, nothing will stop it. If it's not, nothing will save it. Man proposes, Byline. God disposes."

The Truth of Confessions

The new sycamores hold their haughty colors against the approaching season, but the older trees on the ridge are already stripped to their veins by wind or willful release. And the ridge drops off in our back yard not 160 feet, like I said, but more like 240 feet. A tree at the top would fall end-over-end three times before smashing on the rocks.

I don't know what to do with the passing of these autumn days, so I make stabs at understanding, grabs at precision, in the hope of making a connection.

The first thing I did when I got home from St. Francis was play a message back on the machine, and what a foul thing it was to hear Charlie Gul's voice on the recording say "I'm here...and you're here."

He said it with the drunken pride of irreverence. He swilled the words on purpose.

I woke up the next morning with the words in my ear *'Have you found me, O my enemy?'* But I don't know if C-Gul has found me or not. If he came to the suburbs to hunt me, he would have had me by now. He wants his money. He can have his money. In seven thousand installments. Money is all he has over me anymore. Money and the trick of making questions seem like indictments – his biggest one being *Quo Vadis*.

Disgust still stews in me from the night I learned what Charlie Gul actually taught. He actually taught that when a believer metabolizes booze, the process releases *molecules of God*. There was a whole litany that C-Gul invoked to go along with it that said by exhaling spirit bits you could liberate limited thinking, and that sex in this state could propagate the faith, and that the seat of wisdom was in the pubis.

He would don that doctrine all night until he got one of the 7th Avenue girls into bed. I was somehow preserved those nights from getting naked with any of them, except Odessa, who came later and who was never one of the circle jerks. I was saved from the act. And the fact is that sex for its own sake isolates desire from everything else about the girl. Crash intercourse doesn't serve love and it's the truth whether you buy it or not. Every time you rip off someone in bed you run a little faster from the louse inside you.

I put the letter to Cicero in the mailbox and watch the 9:24 bus roll away downhill.

That was the last morning peak to Ossining.

The next one will be in an hour.

I had to delay myself with the trees, didn't I? I couldn't recognize I was late and adjust.

I was late because I was writing Cicero's letter. Late because the job will always wait. The newspaper isn't a clock job where you have to be there at the split of nine. But they do expect you by 10:30 or so. It's people like me who aren't in the business for the career who drag down the profession to its sub standards, the same way waiters run restaurants into the bin for the chefs who are trying to *do* something with food. The poor professionals in journalism and restaurants do their best to sidestep the scandal that the rest of us cause, but no amount of grad school polish or downtown work ethic can change the fact that they are both businesses of slipping standards. From the beginning.

The sun rides me hard as I trudge west on the highway shoulder towards the Hudson River. A silvery Volvo smokes by, and I picture my editor Phyllis Stein handing me my ass this time.

To think I just mailed that puffed-up letter to Cicero about how this separation has been 'beneficial, even inspirational.'

Ah, pride, what a thing! No matter how you dirty it with toil in restaurants and newsrooms, it climbs up from the soil in royal clothes, wanting respect. It tells you you're unique. That you're as good as you imagine. The best who ever was. It tags along with you into sobriety. Into pews. Pride gives you permission to settle for less in your pockets than the immigrants because that is what Jesus did. Who can bear it!

Out of town, the asphalt shoulder gives to dirt, and the dirt narrows to nothing. Banks steep on both sides, so that I'm forced to walk on the road. I shift my black bag to the other hand each 100 feet now, since both arms are tired of carrying it, making my back strain to compensate.

It's no good. I'm a bum in a land of chrome-trimmed chariots.

I give up.

I sit at the next stop and wait for the damn bus.

When I do get to the office, my problem is not that I am late. My problem is that I am not on the bib with a story for tomorrow's paper. We call the daily storyboard a bib because if we don't feed the editors copy, they cry like babies. Mondays are like that. I figure if I get desperate I'll find stories off the college security office blotter. Some campus party bust. Carthage College and Ossining's west bank is my beat. The other reporters figure they'll scrounge something off their beats on Monday as well, so when Phyllis Stein has a clean bib at the Monday morning feeding meeting with the bureau chiefs, it puts her in a vile temper.

Usually I can find a good campus story on Monday, but since I sheared the Parisienne, the bus takes forever between the office and the west bank. I've had to work the phone, which is not my strength.

My desk is against a plate window that never gets cleaned, and my view of the Hudson River is blocked by Sing Sing: an olive-gray curtain of cement and parapets with curly-qued barbed wire slinked along the top. Here comes the execution mail I've been expecting, across the top of my computer screen, in two words: "See me." Phyllis Stein is finished with the morning conference call, and she wants to know what I've got.

"I haven't gotten to my rounds," I tell her. She's done something to her hair again. It's darker and sharper.

"Shut the door." She's wearing a three-quarter length black cardigan and a purple scarf as high as a turtleneck. Her chest line is open past the breast cleft to the immodest third button of her blouse. The woman has got to be 60 years old.

"What's going on with you, Dante?" She uses a motherly tone that makes me give a quick thought to the idea of trusting her.

The red spider vein in Phyllis Stein's left nostril looks inflamed as though it will pop, but it won't pop. The last time it looked this red she was hot about the abortion pictures she got in the mail the day after I featured the Sanger Center, which had just rented the old movie house on the river. I didn't know the Sanger Center did abortions. I thought it was a health clinic.

Someone sent pictures of mauled up babies with their legs torn off and their torsos disemboweled and their chests charcoal-black with saline burns. Babies in unborn skin with white mouths frozen open in a shouting shape. It seared a sore in my brain where the things flash back before I can stop them. I agreed at the time with Phyllis Stein's point that the sickest part about the pictures was that fanatics would send them at all.

But that's not it. The sickest thing about abortion is that it looks you in the eye, so that you know exactly what it is, and you either have to get rid of it or let it torture you, even though in all honesty, there is nowhere in the universe to throw it away.

"Dante?" She's playing psychologist.

"Nothing's wrong," I tell her.

"What are you doing for tomorrow?"

"I'll find something."

"Where? In *Adeo*?"

Witch. *Adeo* is the Carthage College weekly, and lately I've been beat by them — not on anything major.

"Bobby, this isn't you."

I don't trust her. I've never trusted her. She's told me to bring wine and flowers to interviews to improve my rapport. She once told me 'Dress gay. I don't mean fruit gay. I mean good gay. Goldenrod. Violet. I don't care. But get the *hang* of it.'

"What's this about you not having a car?"

Damn. I told one guy in the newsroom about Dickens.

"I have a car."

"Show me where it's parked."

"It got in an accident."

"Fix it."

"I can't afford to right now."

"It's a job requirement. You need a car. You've been slipping and I've let it go. You blow deadline. You pile up corrections. You miss staff meetings. I tell you to do something and you ignore me and say you forget. You don't forget. You don't respect me? I have a plan for that. I don't respect you. I don't want to be surprised by an undergrad rag. We're a newspaper, Dante. Either get me good stories or get lost. And get a new prosthesis. That *thing* is so unprofessional.

"Okay."

"What did you say?"

She's shocked that I acquiesced. So am I. It wasn't as hard as I thought it would be. And it has lightened the atmosphere.

"Look, you're a quick study and you're organized and you're one of my better reporters. I like the chances you take in your copy when they work. But you don't communicate with me."

"If I told you what I was going through – " I look into the framed poster of the 27th annual United Nations Women in Development Conference, where Phyllis Stein was a roundtable headliner, and I stop myself from finishing. I would tell her about AA if it felt like the right thing to do, but it doesn't.

This isn't the ideal world where the truth sets you free. This is the stage where the truth serves the cause. And the last thing you do on stage is drop the act. You'll never be in another play.

I'm surprised by how depressing this is. I'm tempted to tell her about AA against my judgment, but I don't, and I feel dismay rushing to the surface. I smother the tears with a grimace, shaking my head 'no.' Phyllis Stein withdraws a tissue that I didn't see in time.

"Anybody can figure out that you are going through something," she says. "And I feel sorry for you. But you don't talk to me, so I don't like you. People will help you, but they have to like you."

"Okay."

"You need a car to keep the job."

"Okay."

"You need good stories to keep this job."

"I know."

"Who's that guy out there?"

"Where?"

"The Hare Krishna on the loading dock. He says he has a tip for you. But I don't believe him. He's a friend of yours, isn't he? See what he wants and then go to Carthage. Find me something. I don't need anything from you for tomorrow, but I need something good for the weekend. And don't turn your back on me, because turning your back on me is the same thing as walking out on me."

"I thought you were done."

"I'm not. I want you to smile."

"Okay."

"Dante."

"What?"

"Now. I want you to smile now. And from now on."

I think she just asked me to do the hardest thing in the world. My face muscles can't pull it off. She jaws at me as I leave, but her telephone rings, and I know she won't chase me.

I follow the reek of Ori's shit cigar to the production bays where the gulls fight for air rights over the Dumpsters. The skyscape extends beyond Sing Sing to the timber-green Hudson Highlands.

Ori is wearing a salmon-colored poncho and faded baggy jeans that give his getup a robe look like a Krishna, except for his dark shades and rolled up *Lancet*.

"They're working with engrams in the hippocampus, Byline. A new pathway to imprints in the womb. Can you imagine?"

I sail a salute over my head to show him that he's talking above me again. It's the quickest way to make him define his terms.

"The area deep in the forebrain Byline that regulates emotion and memory. The *limbic* system. Didn't they teach you anything in St. Louis? Think memory codes. With trauma. In the *womb*. How does that happen, Byline? Who ever heard of trauma in the womb?"

He's mimicking the gulls with his arms spread high and his poncho wings catching the breeze — breeze that carries the first real chill of autumn.

"Nobody," I tell him.

"But they *found* it." He's waving the rolled up *Lancet* at me. "Where does the trauma come from if it doesn't come from the woman, right?"

"Right."

"The kid is down there at week 18 or 20 and the woman is saying 'I don't want a *kid* with this guy.' Right?"

"Yeah." He's right. But he didn't come out here to tell me about that. He's leaving. I can tell.

"Listen, I didn't come by to tell you about that." Ori lets the wind out of his wings and tucks the journal in his back pocket.

"How's your Latin."

"Rusty, Byline. What's that?"

"Something I found in Cicero's drawers." I show Origen the card with the six Latin words in Old English calligraphy that I ripped out of Cicero's frame. It says: Ratio quasi quadeam lux lumenque vitae.

"That's 'life,'" he says, pointing the Churchill between his middle and fore fingers.

"And that one's 'happy,' obviously. Don't quote me, but that could be, like, tranquility. That's the best I can do."

"It doesn't make any sense."

"To you, Byline."

"To you either. Can't you do better than that?"

"You're a reporter and you can't look it up? I can't crack the oracle every time, Byline. No one can. Anyway, I didn't come for that."

He doesn't say anything. So I ask. "Why do you want to go do this?"

"I haven't told you anything yet."

"Why do you want to go cut yourself off from everything? You know exactly what I'm talking about."

"Because I know what's going to happen before it happens, Byline. It's a curse. But we're not talking about the same thing."

"What are we talking about?"

"Pete the Breeze. Expired. I didn't see you Saturday night at the theater. I figured maybe you didn't hear. Sorry, Byline."

"What do you mean? He's dead?"

"Pretty safe bet, Byline, yeah, otherwise the family reaction would be a tad severe."

Something angry is churning inside Origen.

The black, small shadows of two men appear on the Sing Sing catwalk.

Origen's hostility is accumulating: I can see it hardening on his shaved temple.

"How?" I ask.

"How it always happens, but I only heard it through the keyhole. The family is doing what families do. No funeral. They are calling it a memorial."

"What do you mean no funeral?"

"No casket, Byline. Figure it out."

"Figure what out?" I don't care if he is in a dangerous mood.

"How do you bury a guy with an ice-pick in his head? Come Byline. I thought you knew Pete!"

I knew Pete.

AA worked the same on Pete and me.

We never listened to instruction up to the sixth repetition, but on the seventh pronouncement, brother, we went for the every word.

We swallowed the AA program whole, so that the first 88 pages of AA's Big Book we learned by *clause*, fascinating ourselves and showing up our Program brethren with the applications we drew from words like 'must,' and 'action' and 'promise.'

We quoted the Big Book with the force of Scripture with verses like 'sobriety is not enough' and 'the spiritual life is not a theory.'

But lately Pete's been saying things like 'Yeah? Who's says you can't?" when I say 'You can't take it with you.'

I didn't know Pete.

"What else did you hear?" I mean about how Pete did it.

"One o'clock at St. Francis. Today."

"The thing is today?"

Something in me doesn't want to say goodbye to Breeze. I can't pull it off. I'm trying to figure when it was that Pete started pulling away.

"It's untreated depression," I tell Origen. "When you take the booze away. You gotta fill that hole with God."

"No, Byline, you have fill the hole with love."

"Same thing."

"Touch is the key. It's the *connection.* You can spray your theological libations like a sprinkler in the suburbs, but if you never touch anything you die in the desert."

"You can touch God on a mountain by yourself."

"But I am not on a mountain by myself, Byline. And yet I am. Every night in the rooms with the friends of Job who feed me the coupon creed because they don't want to connect. They don't want to connect because that's where they got knifed the last time, even while their lips say '*I care.*' They don't dare."

"God didn't make the heart to be satisfied with people's love."

"Bullshit, Byline."

"Augustine says our hearts are restless until they rest in God."

"Who says '*You see my calamity and you are afraid*?' Tell me. You want to coupon me, Byline? You win and I die. You've got a kid and a wife and I've got friends of Job. Maybe I could've had kids, but it's not in the cards anymore. I tell people I'm better off being a fucking eunuch and they look at me like *this.*"

Ori wrinkles his brow in mock confusion and makes an 'O' shape with his scarred lips. "People don't get it."

"You expect people to *get* that?"

"If I see someone I like, and she sees me, we both know the imprint before a word. Am I making myself clear? It's the pattern. The engram. There's a time when I said, 'Hey, maybe it can work out with this one. Maybe she's the cure. I'll have some fun before the veil rips. But the woman isn't the cure, she's the injury. Come on, Byline! *'Teach me and I'll be silent. How forceful are honest words!*'"

The two dark figures on the catwalk must be guards, not inmates, because they are outside the wire.

I could beg Ori to stay in New York and I could divert him from dire thoughts, but there's a point where he has to be tried by his own ideas. And he's past that point right now, talking old history about how scientifically significant it was to sodomize Cara Kole, because it represents a *mark*.

It doesn't represent anything. It only cowers to Origen's case that man is a herd animal.

I argue that for a man who mounts such an enormous fight for science as the rule of life, science ought to serve him better in the clutch.

And at least let him keep his balls.

"Some of us choose death, Byline. Some of us have it chosen for us."

I don't know what he's talking about, but he's got me on ice. He's about to spin me with something.

"When she got pregnant, she told me what she was going to do."

"Cara Kole was pregnant?"

"Because she couldn't be touched."

"You never told me that."

"Murder."

"You had an abortion?"

"*Mur-der.*"

"Wait a minute, Origen."

"The second time she didn't tell me. She just did it."

"Back up a second, Ori.

"*Muur-derr.*" His lips are gorged like erectile tissue. The word consumes his whole mouth.

"Origen, she had two abortions?"

"Two months after that, nothing was left but to leave."

"Did you tell your sponsor?"

Ori looks past the guards in prison towards the Highlands.

He didn't tell his sponsor.

I know my jaw is hung open, but I don't do anything to close it because he is looking inward.

Anyway why should I? This dissenter who keeps the Program honest with his Thesis has an invalid fourth step! He has to start the whole Program over. He's known it from the beginning. Now so do I.

"Look, Byline. I came to tell you about the Breeze. I'm sorry for this. I wanted to tell you something else, but I don't have the heart now."

"Don't you believe — "

"I don't believe, Byline."

"Then don't you know that God forgives?"

"No, Byline. What I know is *'If someone is burdened with the blood of another, let that killer be a fugitive until death.'*"

Proverbs remind me of my mother. She never had a whisper of wisdom to share with me in St. Louis, but now that she's gone, she's a regular

Queen of Sheba. Somebody should tell her that her scripture is out of season.

She ought to hold her peace, which is exactly what I am going to do with Origen, because there is nothing I can say to the wind anyway.

Nothing I can do but to let him go, his poncho flaps swept by the spirit.

The two guards have turned the corner where a turreted tower is cantilevered into the skyscape. They disappear into the clouds.

So much of what has confused me about Origen is clearing.

This is why fatherhood is always a taboo with him. Not only his old man's but his own.

It's why he's obsessed with Marco's origin.

Ori's revelation has exposed his motivation.

It explains his hostility to marriage, his certainty that he'll never have the new woman because of what happened with the old woman. It explains how he can harbor heresy about a God whose reach can't touch and whose touch can't connect.

Origen's solution is ingenious: his balls are his kids. One testicle for each abortion.

And the Golden Gate Bridge — what a stage!

It's not a plunge, but a launch. No more sex drive, no more dead offspring. And his penance is paid, as long as at least one person knows it.

It's the only reason he told me.

At last I have something to work with. The only medicine for a condemned heart is mercy. And no one administers mercy like God.

It doesn't occur to me until after I reach the end of the street, where a 60-foot-high retaining wall is testament to how much river bank they excavated to build Sing Sing, that I can tolerate Seagull's stalking, and Pete's suicide, and Phyllis Stein's ultimatum, and Cicero's refusal to answer my letters because I have something up on Ori now.

For all my trouble, I have a cleaner Program than he does, even if I haven't finished it.

Sixty feet down, the women wait for their husbands to get off guard duty.

They have their campers and RV's and rusted mobile home trailers lined up against Sing Sing's great wall, across the gully, with their awnings pitched and their propane tanks out and their doors open to the overcast cold, while fast food wrapper garbage runs circles with the first fallen leaves.

The women camp out here because sometimes 12 hours is all their husbands get off before they return to duty. The guards are like nurses in that way, with back-to-back shifts, and it's the most incredible thing about Sing Sing if you ask me — not so much that the top security prison north of Rikers Island allows a trailer park inside the compound — but that the women do it at all. They camp out for days, just to get that 12 hours with their men, because it is worth it.

Cissy used to camp out in the church parking lot after the AA meetings and wait for me, a little too eager to show herself waiting, until I snapped at her in front of everyone that the Al-Anon meeting was at the Y. It was awful to do to her.

Cissy was good to me. She was as good as one of these trailer women.

I want her back.

I ache for her in my throat and in my chest. I can't stop reading from the poem I found in her drawer the Sunday she left with Marco:

When I was little
I sometimes woke alone
At night in fear.
The darkness pressed
And I never named my fear
For it had no name or form.
And I never cried or called
For who would hear?
But my fear?
Now I am old
And still the darkness presses,
But inside me:
The darkness of the empty soul.
And now I cry out
And hope
That someone will hear
And calm my fear.
I did what I had to do to stay alive.

Only the last line of the poem is hers. She hand-wrote it.

It makes me think so differently about her and what happened in Muskegon when she was 16. What she had to do to survive.

She got angry at God for letting her get raped and she took it out on the church. Psychology put her life back into secular shape. But she's not an enemy of faith. She's a candidate for it.

I would call her right now if she wasn't in school and tell her I was wrong to insist on bed positions when she told me she couldn't block out Muskegon. Sometimes you choose death, and sometimes you have death chosen for you. Cicero survived when they wanted her dead. Marco outlived the date Odessa and I put on his head. God was there in those moments to show he's there in all moments.

After work, when the bus pulls into the market depot in Mount Kisco, I realize that it wasn't my best response when Origen told me about the abortions to drop my mouth open.

But when I look through Ori's apartment window after knocking on the glass pane, I see something worse.

His banker's boxes are there against the chipped plaster wall, full of his files for the book that he is always never writing, but Ori for once isn't home.

Downstairs, underneath Ori's crap flat, is a brick storefront with 'The Village Tabard' in raised letters over the French panel door, and 'Gourmet Foods and Take Away" stenciled as an afterthought in flat brown paint.

The owner Barnes will know where Ori is.

But Barnes isn't here. It's 6 o'clock in an open restaurant and there is no sign of a waiter, let alone a proprietor.

His window display is three dusty boxes of Droste Cocoa, four bottles of TTG White Cooking Wine, and a magnum of Martinelli sparkling cider.

The wall shelves behind the counter display bulk-ordered kitchen stock — six cans of Savarin coffee, a case of stacked Carr's crackers, a column of Hot Mex salsa bottles, four pillow-sized bags of

Dirty Luther's long-grain rice, and a 12-pack of blue Barilla rotini boxes.

This is Barnes' idea of café decor.

He's out of his little English mind.

Origen won't let me disparage Barnes, because Ori thinks Barnes is a self-defense act, but Origen isn't here. No one is.

You can see the joint is empty from the street.

People don't want to eat in empty restaurants. If you're smart, you shade the windows. Barnes' stupidity makes me want to hurt him by flipping a table, but the tables aren't even set. I would steal money to punish him if I thought there was bread to lift in that register.

I despise him because I have never told him how despicable he is.

"Barnes!"

He must be in the basement.

Outside, across the street, a thin man lights a cigarette that glows orange and then blacks out.

The guy has just come out of a Sanger Center satellite to an alley that never drains where they park the white biohazard boxes.

He is cut clean with a red power tie and rolled up shirt sleeves. Maybe another night he might prop his foot up on a biohazard box for better street posture. But not tonight. He's thinking.

He's thinking nobody is watching him.

What a sucker. The whole world watches you.

"Barnes!"

I hear something faint and sweet. It's a radio, getting louder. It's a National Public Radio recording I think. And a trudge noise on the steps. Barnes is ascending.

"Barnes?"

There follows an unacceptable lapse from Barnes in the kitchen; he makes nothing of his obligation to answer his name.

The lapse is at the center of my disdain for Barnes. His flagging nature is a disguise, because I have seen him snap off his own customers when it suits him. When he isn't in the mood. Whenever he feels threatened.

The bad attitude apparently started with some ringed women from Pound Ridge who he refused to serve. It grew into a skill, so that people sit here today with menus in their hands and he'll tell their astonished faces what he will and will not prepare.

Fine. Barnes won't visit the call, I'll visit Barnes.

I duck under the counter and turn into the kitchen. It's crawl-space dark, because of the low ceiling, and cluttered in both aisles with unpacked leaf greens in waxed boxes.

I'm shocked by the sight of Barnes on his toes with his hips against the stainless steel sink, holding his penis over the edge, the water running hard.

He's pissing.

"Barnes!"

Barnes doesn't jitter. A violin concerto jams from his little radio.

This is absolutely surreal.

Suddenly it strikes me what to do. I hiss over the wailing strings.

"Hey, *you*!"

That twists his neck, so that I am eyed up with the little Englishman. He's wearing a skull-tight pink baseball cap with an elongated bill. The little man drops his face and humpfs something angry that gets lost in the concerto, which I could be wrong about. I get violins and cellos mixed up.

"Where's Origen?"

Barnes looks out the window over the sink, which gives him no relief, because a brick wall is on the other side of it, and I see in his reflection a pause that might mean he's not sure who I am.

"'E's gone."

"I know that," I tell him. Barnes pulls up a colander of bone white leeks from the basin and turns off the water. What was he doing, *blanching* them?

"Then why osk?" He says it timidly.

"I want to know where he is."

Barnes shakes out the colander. Laggard dick. He's not as dilatory as he pretends. His slow pace is a defense against swift thinking, and it won't work. The only reason I haven't gutted him for his insolence is I see a response coming on the bridge of his grey eyes.

"The desert." Barnes acts as if he is surprised himself. I wasn't expecting that. I was expecting him to ask if he was his brother's keeper.

"Which desert?"

"The Chihuahuan."

Origen flew to Frisco. I don't know why I didn't see that coming.

Ori must have gotten on the train to the airport after I saw him. Now I am sorry I didn't tell him that the hard part about the abortions was over with the confession.

I should've told him I feel the same way over Marco. It could have helped Origen off the hook.

I thought I had time with Origen. *God.*

If I think all the time about how I wanted Marco dead in the womb and my wishes were overwhelmed, how much more does Origen think about his dead kids, and his will denied?

I hope Barnes knows what he's talking about.

I hope Origen is on a plane and not tied to three bricks at the bottom of the Hudson River.

I want to make sure that Barnes has his full inventory of knives — at least it would rule something out. Though I don't know what comes after that.

"What did he say?" I ask Barnes.

"Sigh?" He dumps the leeks onto an oak cutting board. A nice one.

"Stop that," I order him. "You're not doing anything with those." I mean the leeks.

"Whad 'e sigh?"

"Right." Let's see if he knows what he's doing or not.

"Stah-ting when?"

I take three steps at Barnes and stop at the range. It bothers me that Origen let this wanker in on his plans and not me.

"Do I look friendly?"

"Yew wan me to on-sur that?" He looks afraid of me, the way I want him to, but he gave me a gutsy answer.

"No," I decide. "He just...he wasn't in good shape this morning."

"Not 'appy."

"Right."

"The lowliest of pursuits — 'appiness."

Barnes is apparently going to make soup. Not that it would be ready now. But maybe he has a catering thing tomorrow.

I'm not so sure Ori told him anything more than what Barnes told me.

That line about happiness being the lowliest of pursuits is an old Origen line, and I need to figure out what I am going to do now.

I was actually thinking of talking out my strategy about Cicero with him, because it needs a good devil's advocate.

I leave Barnes at his cutting board and see that the man in the shirt sleeves is still there in the wet alley. Smoking.

I'm better than that guy. Not because of what I've done, but in spite of what I did. Not better because I'm smarter, but because I'm smaller. I'm smaller in my own eyes. And it's not because I want to be, but because I have to be.

I either live small this way or I die being the big guy.

That's it.

That's the picture to give up.

That's what I have to do to stay alive.

I give up my big picture for power and profit. I give up the picture in me that I've always held against anyone close to me — the picture of me that no one can name because no one can see it.

"Barnes!" I want to know something.

"Oy!" Barnes appears, but with a Wusthof that puts an edge on his pasty face.

"Don't oy me. When I said 'Hey *you*' in there, what did you hear?"

"I'm *nut* cookin.'"

"I'm not asking you to cook, ass."

"At's yur on-sur, idn't it?" He's annoyed. Let him be annoyed.

"I told you I'm not asking you to cook. I want to know what went through your gulliver when I said 'Hey, *you*!'"

"Aye?"

"What went through your brain that made you answer me, Barnes?"

"Tol you, didn' I?"

It's no use. He thinks I'm trying to get him to cook for me.

I want to know why '*you*' hit him closer to home than his own name.

As soon as I say it, I know the answer.

'*You*' is the name God calls.

The name of every everlasting soul.

It's the only name of consequence because it's the only name we need.

God, if this unbelievable day turns out to have a purpose, that would be remarkable.

Son of Many Tears

I used to go around saying I never saw a burning bush.

It was one of those intellectual dishonesties I practiced to keep the God squad from running their scripture through me when Flaco and the Cords of Falsehood drew ire from the Toll Brothers at the Porticoes on York.

The Toll Brothers were Baptists with a storefront church in Hell's Kitchen. The same five of them would hike forty blocks north on Sunday to shout violence at us from Isaiah, calling us 'feet of the foolish' and 'offspring of deceit.'

One Sunday when Flaco's toes were so numb he couldn't walk, I shouted back that I never saw a burning bush, and it shut the Toll Brothers up.

I wasn't only saying I never saw God, I was saying they never saw him, either.

I continued to say it after I got sober, and after I read the Gospels. I said it when I had to start my AA program over with Jared of the Sorrows and the Friday night boys, because I wasn't *getting* the spiritual connection.

I said it to win a nod of affirmation, or to drop a tongue before it rolled over me.

But I was wrong.

I *have* seen a burning bush.

The voice in the garden taught me that.

But I'm not talking about the voice in the garden.

I'm talking about the December 4th sun, two days ago, just above the capillaries of the winter trees.

I was on the bus, riding past the shadow-bar forest on Crow Hill Road, and I looked up at the sun, dancing with glorious white color. It was blinding white but possible still to look on it, and there was an ivory crescent of metallic luster at the bottom. The color of the sun was pure white with no yellow at all.

It was the kind of white that you pollute with description, the kind of white you don't ever see, although you know that you are seeing it.

The more the sun danced the more I believed. And the more I believed the closer I felt drawn. I felt favor, and the feeling didn't fade the way my peace went to vapor watching the bell tower at Goloborza.

The peace didn't go away until I knew what to do; I never would have agreed to make amends to Odessa on my own. It took a burning bush to do that.

It's 2:30 and I'm early.

The entrance ground of the convent is as wide as a golf course and sited on a slope.

Beyond the lawn crown of pine tips is the open valley vista of the Hudson River.

Once again, I'm brought to the river. In August it was Goloborza and God in the garden. In October it was Sing-Sing and Origen. Last week it was West Point and Marco. And today, it's the Poor Clares and Odessa.

Marco was on a mission to get me to Thanksgiving dinner last week at the Major and Mrs. Cruz's, but I had to work that day, so I went up to West Point the next morning to be with him.

Marco led me to a grassed-over redoubt where we sat on cannons and watched the Hudson bend its massive neck around Lookout Mountain and roll past us to the ocean. Cicero looked tired. She said my sister had called her early from Leeds to ask why we weren't back together.

"Her question," Cissy said.

I would've told Cicero that there was no reason I saw for us to stay apart if I would have realized that she was asking me the question herself, and not merely relaying what my sister said.

As it was, I figured I didn't owe my sister an account, and I shrugged it off without answering the question. Dumb.

You can't see anything from here, except the crushed rock path laid over the hill.

I've been here once, years ago when Marco was a baby, and I have a bleary memory that it was a day I should regret.

I'll make small talk with Odessa about Marco, tell her she looks good, and then give her my speech: *I'm sorry. I know what I did was wrong. I knew it was wrong when I did it. I blamed you for the mistakes I made, and when you kept Marco, I abandoned you. I abandoned him. Will you forgive me for that? Will you let me make it up to you?*

I'm going to keep it short. Jared says a ninth step that lingers past the facts is self-indulgent.

God knows this has to be a clean confession, with no self-serving and no finger-pointing, if I want to shake free.

The beauty of this step is that Odessa doesn't have to forgive me.

As long as I ask for her peace, I have done everything in my power. The rest is up to her, and I can be free.

I'm shivering like a freshman at a football game. It must be 30 degrees, and I still have a long way to walk. We used to pour Peppermint Schnapps in hot chocolate and put our hands up the sweaters of the Trinity girls in the locker room under the football stadium during Saturday home games. What happened to those days? What happened to me?

I see the first mansard roof and the cap of a ribbed gold dome up river.

When I called Odessa and told her I wanted to apologize she said don't bother. Her voice was raw like she'd been sucking lemon, but I persisted.

She said "Okay, Bub," in a throaty tone that I never heard from her. She didn't sound like 90 pounds on the phone. She sounded sultry.

I swing between projections of intrigue and horror.

This is the bitch who blinded me and entrapped me and held me hostage with a six-year secret that ruined me.

But I have to stop taking counsel in my fear. I have to do something to climb out of this unbelievable hole before someone forgets I'm in here and fills it.

The mansard roof turns out to be a carriage house.

The convent is in a slate blue Gothic Revival castle with a square-tooth battlement roof and a cone spire tower, built by some turn-of-the-century financier.

The infirmary is supposed to be a new brick building, but I don't see it.

Another Gothic monstrosity with steep pitched roofs, gargoyles and an ornate blood-red Victorian porch guards a garden of old evergreens.

Up river is the gold-dome chapel with its stained glass windows, stone column sculptures and vaulted double-door entrance.

Can this all be the Poor Clares?

There is a nun my mother's age on the spiral stairs in the convent foyer, who is probably not the right one to ask for directions, because at the desk near the fireplace beyond the suspended life-size crucifix, a black girl in a novice habit is manning what looks like a receptionist telephone.

"I was looking for the infirmary," I tell the sister, because she was staring at me and making me self-conscious. I'm dressed *fine*. Black turtle neck sweater, jeans that are ripped in the knee but clean, a sheepskin coat that's stained but not cheap. I could have shaved. "For Odessa Cruz."

"Oh."

"She's my sister-in-law."

"Oh."

"She told me where to go, but I forgot."

"I know you."

Oh no. Something is coming back to me.

"You visited us before, didn't you?" She's coming down the steps. "When the boy was a baby."

I'm looking at her with all the seriousness I can throw forward in the hope of remembering what I did that day: I was laughing-high, and there was some joke about my cigarette, but that's all that's coming to me.

"I'm sorry," I tell her.

"Don't be," she says. Her habit is the color of a fawn. "Don't stay away so long next time. The elevator is this way."

In the elevator is a nun of my grandmother's age who I get introduced to by the younger nun as "Marco's *uncle.*"

"Oh," says the grandmother nun. She looks serious first, probably because the younger sister put such emphasis on the word uncle. Why did she? The grandmother nun finally nods and latches the iron gate.

Now I'm alone in a closet-sized elevator with the sister as old as my grandmother who sits on her stool, minding her business, but giving me the feeling she knows something.

I suppose Odessa told these nuns everything.

When the door opens, a sister in her nineties steps in hunched down, with a black sweater over her habit in the fashion of Mother Teresa. My introduction again is "Marco's *uncle.*"

The nun in her nineties doesn't look serious before she smiles, but I do: I don't like the way it sounds.

The grandmother nun exits, snapping the metal gate shut. My old escort pushes the fifth floor button. That's where I'm going. But mercy, this thing is slow. I need to get out of here. What's that? The elevator has jerked stop.

"Oh it does that." Now there's no motion except the nun's nodding.

"I, ah — " I stop because I can't think what to say. She expects me to speak. *Say anything.* "I may join the Catholic church someday."

"Oh."

Why did I say that? The elevator jerks on.

"Well." She's smiling because this is her territory and I'm trapped. "I'm sure the church would be very happy to have you."

The doors open and I unlatch the iron gate myself.

What possesses me to say these things?

I follow the corridor bridge over the courtyard and into the infirmary.

When Odessa said the infirmary was modern, I pictured something built recently. This was modern in the 1960s. It looks more like a condominium, with Oriental carpets and broad-leafed plants in Tuscany bowls and tapestries on the wall of Jesus and St. Francis and St. Clare. The African girl who shows me to Odessa's room speaks Oxford English and has the same habit as the black girl at the desk.

I have forgotten how nervous I am. Why didn't I bring flowers?

The novice knocks open the white door just enough to put her head through. "Odessa, a handsome man is here for you." She says it loud enough for everyone on the floor to hear. Then the African girl says: "Okay, go."

Odessa swings her wide, dark eyes on me, but she holds her round chin in profile, without smiling.

I gaze on the pleasing scape of her China doll cheek and regal black hair, softened with a white cloth head scarf and waved over her ear with a salon curl.

I look on the mount of her Mongolian lips, round as marble, and I wonder if she has spent the last three years in plastic surgery.

No one has said anything. Odessa hasn't smiled. She's never had to.

Odessa sits in a stiff 'L' position in bed, with sheets up to her waist and a navy blue sweatshirt that says ARMY in yellow letters across the chest. Her far arm — her right arm — is hooked to a Korean War-era IV stand, thick as a street lamp, and there are pictures of Jesus, Mary, and the saints on her headboard and walls. She has a full window view of the muddy green Hudson River and a fireplace with a paisley red love seat and two rocking chairs. Marco's bed with his Noah's Ark covers is angled in one corner near a computer, and there is a kitchen counter by Odessa's bed that is lined with tea tins, old apple sauce jars of mushrooms, fungus and herbs, and a brown brew of leaves and bark in a glass pitcher.

"Home." She says. She isn't smiling.

I'm not moving because she's not letting me. The far side of her face — the right side — is where the scars are. And they are as bad as any scars you have ever seen. The grafts look like skin off the bottom of your feet, and the pocks where the stitches checked betray her refinement with an embattled look. She accepted it. She was tough as the cross about it.

What does she think, I've forgotten, and we'll just keep the conversation on her good side? Wait a minute. She's looking at my patch.

"You know what this is?" I mean to speak humorously about how I cut it out of Cicero's bra, but I stop myself, because I don't want Odessa to take it like I'm pointing out that she blinded me. I'm not.

Once again I have to finish something I started that I can't get out of. Stupid.

It occurs to me that in spite of Odessa's bad breaks, her profile could still turn 10 heads in 10 seconds on Broadway, and snap a few heads right off their loser necks.

"You look so well," I tell her.

"That's what people always say."

"People are right."

"To make themselves feel good." I get her chin when she says it.

"To make you feel good you mean."

"How? By telling me something to my face that they would never say behind my back?"

"No one's allowed to be nice?"

"No one's allowed to lie."

Listen to how Odessa has changed. No one's allowed to flatter her? This is a girl who lived for that.

I'm not going to let her win the point just because she's dying.

"I don't lie, and I say you look good. You look great. And you know what else? I'm going to walk right over there and check out your view."

"Fine, go ahead."

Suddenly I wish I hadn't said that. I see Marco's Raymond Owl stuffed animal on his rocking chair.

This is all Odessa has left of her life.

"Whenever ... you're ready," I say. And it sounds stupid as soon as I say it.

"Ready for what?"

See? Stupid. Say something bright. Save yourself. For her sake: "Ready to give me the grand tour."

"Oh. I don't do tours anymore." She points to the IV.

I sit in a high-armed black leather chair that doesn't go with the rest of the room. I imagine Odessa had the novice put here for me.

"You know what the problem is with a chair like this?" I tell her.

"No."

"Once you sit down, you can't get up."

"I know you better than that, Bub."

This small talk sucks. Better to bag it and stick to the plan.

"What plan?" She says.

"Was I talking to myself? It's gotten worse since I got sober. I have this *thing* where as soon as I start thinking too hard my lips move and I don't realize what I'm doing. "Was I talking or were my lips just moving?"

She's looking away at something on her table, and reaching across her body with her left hand, over her bandaged right arm.

She has a little white paper cup with pill shadows in it. When she twisted, her sweatshirt raised, and I saw the catheter taped to her concentration camp back.

I shiver with the chill I get when I identify with the pitiful effort that people make to be liked.

I imagine the nuns bouffing Odessa's hair and making her bed shine and telling her 'wait 'till he sees you.' I tried to tell her she looked great, but she didn't want to hear it.

God, she swallowed those pills dry like they were nothing.

"Marco knows a lot about West Point," I tell her.

"Was he good?"

"He was great. You've done wonders with him. I love his crew cut."

"I was sick about it."

"No, no. He's a handsome kid. He's got that cute little v-plow in front, you know, where the short hair sticks up? We had fun. You'll like this. We were sitting and watching the leaves swirl in their cyclones the way they do, and I said to Marco 'Isn't it interesting how the leaves only dance like that after they've fallen from the tree?'"

"What did he say?"

"I'm trying to think exactly how he put it."

"You didn't weird him out did you?"

"Would I tell you the story if it weirded him out?"

"It weirds me out, Bub."

"You don't see the connection? The leaves fall down dead. But they dance like they never could attached to the tree. I'm not going to argue with you. It was supposed to make him hopeful."

"Did it?"

"He said the leaves on the trees want to

leave so they can dance too — something like that. It was cute."

"He was devastated that you couldn't come for Thanksgiving."

"Devastated is a big word. Devastated is Thanksgiving on the street. Devastated is when your wife leaves you. Marco wasn't devastated. He was disappointed. I told Cissy I had to *work*. I had to cover a shelter where they shoveled grub to the homeless while the press asked single mommy how grateful she was to have sweet potato pie on a plastic plate."

"Marco thought if he asked you, you would come."

"Where? To your old man Steuben's? So he could run me through?"

"We had it here."

"You had Thanksgiving dinner here? Cicero came here?"

"We thought if Marco asked you, you would come."

"Maybe you shouldn't have sent a five-year-old to do a grown-up's job. Anyway I don't believe Cicero was here."

"How do you think Marco got here?"

"Your old man. Or Emily."

"I never wanted Emily near him. I still don't."

"That's how it is."

"I want you to take Marco back."

"Now you ask, after everything is ruined."

"He's not going to kill you." She means Brutus. Now I'm worried.

"So he knows?"

"He's been prepared. Emily knows. She's

been preparing him."

"How does Emily know?"

"I told her," Odessa says.

"You told her!" That's a lie.

"She asked me."

"You're lying."

"She said Cicero knew, so what could I say?"

"You told her about Quo Vadis?" I point to my eye.

"Who are you shouting at? You *used* me."

"You used me."

"I was a *girl*."

"Did you tell her about Quo Vadis or not?"

"Listen, Bub — "

"Why would you tell someone you despise?"

"She made it easy."

"How!"

"She's a woman."

"So Steuben doesn't know?" I want a straight answer.

"He knows."

"What are you smiling at?" I've been waiting to see Odessa smile, but not at my expense like this.

"Nothing. Sorry."

"No, go ahead. What?"

"He still wants to wrestle you."

"Let me tell you something. I was twenty seven-and-two my senior year. Practically undefeated."

"So was he. You should see his pictures."

I picture Brutus in a torso suit from the black-and-white 1940s with a concept of wrestling that's no more refined than low-class ring fighting. That's where I'll beat him. You can have 190 pounds of muscle, but you'll be on your back counting ceiling stars if you don't have *technique.*

"A man his age can get hurt pretending he's in high school." I'm serious, but Odessa holds her smile in profile with her half-moon eye and pan-shaped cheek. I see her compensating for her right side. She talks like she's had a stroke. It's still a striking smile though, and I can't stay angry, even if she thinks it's funny that her killer father wants to murder me.

I'm not sure what to believe, but maybe Odessa is saying that fearing the worst from Brutus is overkill.

"These your friends?" I point to the icons on the wall. I want to keep her smiling. She's also got holy cards hole-punched and tied with red ribbons to her bed handles and IV stand. There must be thirty statues of saints on her medicine table and vanity and television.

"My heroes. You know what I'm going to do?"

She's still smiling. I wish I had a camera.

"What?" I ask her.

"I'm going to spend my time in heaven doing good on earth. The Little Flower said that. Isn't that beautiful? You know the Little Flower?"

Actually I do. My mother says she'll be bigger than Joan of Arc.

"Yeah." I sit down in my black chair. "Believe it or not, I do."

Odessa turns to me full face. Her right eye has drooped badly above the patchwork of her reconstructed cheek, but I swear on my wedding ring that there is a fire in her gaze that makes you want to get under her skin.

"Does your mother still write to you, Bub?"

"All the time."

"Does she know how serious you are now?"

"I don't know."

"She would love to know that. If I were her, I would. Maybe she would stop writing so much if she knew. You are very serious now, you know."

Something huge has happened to Odessa. I'm enjoying what's coming out of her mouth and I'm actually giving it weight.

I think about how long Cicero has held me down by saying I'm *not* serious, about anything, including myself, and how that has been a trip wire in our marriage, so that it still makes me wonder whether I'm good enough for her.

Now some bedridden 23-year-old Army brat is telling me that I'm serious.

Suddenly I see someone new in Odessa. Someone I trust. Someone I admire. Someone who values what I'm doing.

This girl is dying and she's picking *me* up.

She does the same crossover drill with her free arm, lifting a paper cup by her thumb and forefinger and knocking back the pills.

God gave Odessa knock out looks and then cast her out of the camp. He gave her a darling boy to love with her broken heart, but God took that away too when she drank a transfusion spiked with the HIV. Yet in Odessa's deathbed disfigurement, she has a gift more resplendent than beauty or motherhood – she has the soul of a saint. And a revelation comes to me that if anybody could understand the voice in the garden, it's her.

She drinks pills like liquid. Three o'clock must be her cocktail hour.

"It's hard to talk about this, because I don't want to sound like God speaks to me, you know?" I wait for her to nod an acknowledgment. But she doesn't. This is an important point, so I go back to it: "I mean, do you believe people who say 'God talks to me?'"

"It depends if I believe them, Bub."

"That's what I mean. Do I look believable?"

"It's not how you look."

"I'm sorry — " I tell her. She's got a paper cup halfway to her mouth. "I didn't mean to stop you."

"I do this every day," she says. "Do you want my answer? You can't make people believe you. People have to choose what to believe. I believe you."

"The worst is now that I've given up my picture, I feel myself reaching back for it, you know?"

She nods, but maybe it's the pills she's knocking back.

"Important thing is that you catch yourself doing it," she says.

"Yeah but sometimes I dream on a little too far and indulge myself."

"Don't be discouraged because you're tempted. Sorry, Bub. I can't think. The Procrit makes me fuzzy."

She rocks her head back and grimaces.

"Are you okay, Odessa?"

"Just once I'd like to take a pill holiday."

Suddenly a thought from the outside drops into my head.

"Do you ever think about eternal life?" I stand to wait for her answer.

"*Oh yeah.*" Her eyes are closed, but she says it with pronouncement.

"I really don't."

"Oh *I* do."

"You do?"

She's looking at me glassy-eyed but sober as Sunday: "*Oh yeah.*"

"I'm just grateful to have a second chance, you know? You know how many times I should have been dead?"

"More than you know, Bub. What's wrong?"

"Nothing. You know, Marco calls me that because of you."

"What do you want him to call you?"

That question still ties me up. I sit back down. Odessa knows I'm not going to answer her.

She closes her eyes again and mouths "Exactly."

A secular nurse in clogs and a business jacket apparently isn't used to the chair here, because she halts when she comes in with a disoriented exasperation, looking at the bed and then my feet.

A thought startles me that Odessa is dead, with her head back, and her lips parted, and her eyelid flat as a coaster. She isn't dead. The nurse was merely perplexed, and now the nurse snatches two Saf-Med gloves from a dispenser on the sink counter and stretches them on. She's strapping Odessa's near arm for a pulse. Fingertips are the only part of the nurse's hand that touch Odessa. If nurses would have shown this much caution with the blood transfusion, Odessa wouldn't be an untouchable.

There is something degrading about the

arm's length way Odessa is being handled.

"How did Cicero look to you?" I ask Odessa. The nurse blocks my view of Odessa and obviously doesn't want small talk while she's working.

Someone needs to teach this nurse the difference between work and service.

"Was she friendly?" I'm talking about Thanksgiving. I picture Cicero being here in body only, staring into the fire. Rubbing her belly.

"She wasn't going to give me a kiss," Odessa says.

"Neither am I." The nurse didn't like that. She huffs around the bed to the IV stand. Odessa didn't like it, either. She's shaking her head at me.

"Don't shake your head at me," I tell her. "What they know about this disease they can spit into the sea. I'll give you a hug. How's that?"

"I don't want a hug from you."

"You can't tell me how my wife looked?"

"Doesn't that question seem funny to you? Ouch."

"Sorry," the nurse says. She looks sorry. I don't know what she did.

Odessa says to her in a completely polite way: "I haven't seen him in a long time. Could this wait?"

The nurse keeps working.

"If I could make Cicero come back I would," I tell Odessa.

"You want to know how she looked?" Odessa says. "She looked like she needed to sleep in her own bed. What's so funny?"

"Nothing. I need her to sleep in her own bed, too."

"You're not a priest, Bub."

"Oh, great," snaps the nurse. She's fed up with us and she sweeps past me, yanking off her rubber gloves.

I look at Odessa and wonder how she knows so much, because she's right.

I have thought about hiding away in a habit and leaving these troubles, but I never pushed the thinking, because you can't become the new man by avoiding the old man. Besides, sleeping alone has been the bleakest part of the separation. I grind my teeth against it every day. I don't know how the nuns and the priests do it.

Odessa is grinning at me. "It only lasts seven seconds you know."

The seven seconds gimmick came from Overeaters Anonymous, where it got started that a hunger pang lasts seven seconds and can be beaten by waiting it out.

I've heard people try to make seven seconds an AA coupon. Ironically what happens is you think how goofy it is to believe you can conquer a disease that kills 9 out of 10 people by counting to seven, and you remember all the other ridiculous quick fixes you never fell for, until you've spent so much time in diversion that you're past the craving.

"You have all the answers now, don't you?" I don't mean it in an ill way. Odessa knows that.

"God, I hope not."

The thought occurs to me to see if she really does have the answers: "What happened with the white light?"

"Why do you call it that?" She looks amused.

"That's what it's called."

"Says who? There was no white light."

"Okay then, a vision."

"It was definitely a vision. See this?" She takes up a micro cassette recorder she has in the covers. Then she reaches across her body again — God! I wish she wouldn't do that. She's going to pull something out.

"Stop. I'll get them."

"I can reach them, Bub. I put them here." She puts a round pink hat box on her lap, displaying fifty micro cassettes fanned in a circle.

"For your memoirs?" I'm kidding.

"For Marco, when he's ready."

"What do they say?"

"Don't test God. Be careful what you ask for. Innocence is eternal."

"I mean about the vision."

"Things you think are problems are the things that protect you."

"What do you mean?"

"Virginity. Modesty..." She's tearing up. "Self-control. I'm sorry."

"It's okay. You drank a lot of pills."

"It's not that, Bobby. You know what it is? I get to say good-bye to him. I'm so lucky. He's so good. So sweet. He's so gentle and so trusting. And all that is going to change the first time he needs me and I'm not there. All that beautiful innocence that would have protected him won't help him. And it's going to hurt him so much when that happens. It hurts me, Bobby. But you know what hurts me more? Do you know what kills me?"

I can't look at her. She's heading straight for the abortion.

"Do you?" She wants me to look at her, but I

won't. "It kills me that if I had my way, he would have been ripped apart alive, in pieces, in my own body, and thrown out like trash. Like garbage. Is he garbage, Bobby?"

I wish she would stop it.

"He's treasure. I wanted to throw away treasure! That's the injustice that kills me! Do you know what I mean? He is so much better than me but he thinks I'm wonderful. He thinks I'm *good*."

She's not accusing me, but I feel accused.

"You know what I mean? God, Bobby! Do you? You must know!"

I get up to leave.

I can't drop my pretenses and collapse into remorse and abandon my defenses to hysterics in public the way she does.

Her wet nose and purple lips and strained throat remind me of my miserable past — the booze-brave night flights, the mornings of cave-sleep, the days of killing time and hiding away for another night to continue the fight.

But this scene here is not like my bad past. Because I am not my past. I am *not* my misery. It took me a year in the Program to separate who I was from what I did and how I felt.

With my hand on the door latch, I realize that I have never accepted my grief over Marco, but I've always turned it away.

And now my tears well up. I feel the same as Odessa about Marco. He's too good for me. I don't deserve him. If he knew who I really was, he would hate me, too.

"When he's not here and I think it looks like a good day to die, I cheer myself up by thinking I still have things to teach him." Odessa has a small red handkerchief that she keeps in the hand of her immobile right arm — the hand she used to blind me. I just saw her grab the handkerchief with her free hand, dab her eyes and return it. "Where are you going, Bub?"

"Nowhere."

"I think of Hannah and I say to myself, 'I've raised a good boy,' you know? At least I have that. But what did I have to do with the *way* he is?"

She means the mother of the prophet Samuel. It's a great analogy, but suddenly it makes me wonder whether she promised Marco to God.

"I can't take any credit," Odessa is sobbing again. "I have nothing to do with his goodness."

"Did you promise God if Marco lived he would be a priest?"

"Bubby, I'm talking about credit for something I didn't do."

She's avoiding the question.

"What about you?" She asks.

"What do I take credit for that I didn't do? I don't know. Being two paychecks away from the day screams on the Bowery I guess."

"That's all?"

"There needs to be more?"

"Much more."

I want to know how this question turned on me: "More than what?"

"More than a savings account against the day screams."

"I don't have a *savings* account."

"In case you were tempted to start one."

The African nun knocks her way in before the last rap fades, dancing to Odessa's bed to draw the sheet off her bony knees for the bed pan.

"I'll wait outside."

"Don't leave," Odessa says.

I walk to the window with my eye on the wall of saints, but as I pass the fireplace I have the surest sense of peripheral movement – a full body!

I whirl and see a rigid horizontal black-suited Madame, bending at the waist and sitting up stiffly, batting her drugged eyes on the damn love seat with her shoes off and holes in her black stockings.

"Jesus!" I shout.

"*Nichego*!" The Madame snarls and rolls her hung-over eyes like I did something to her. Her hair is short as a cap and as white as toothpaste.

"Bobby, my mother is taking a nap."

Odessa is trying to apologize, saying "she has a headache," and "she was up all night," but we are way past the point of sympathy here.

Who does this?

I let my blood boil because I'm justified. Outraged. I'll say it again: when does this ever happen?

"How is your pain, dear?" The novice comes and holds Madame's hand.

I've heard about Madame. I've heard how she can only paint by the Black Sea. How striking she is.

She's got the same Mongol pan face as Odessa, but she's a red drunk.

"*Izvinite*," she murmurs to the novice. "*Prostite menia*."

"Don't be sorry," the African strokes Madame's white hair with her dark fingers. "Lie down," the novice says. "You startled him."

I glare at Odessa because I don't believe this Madame is sorry about spying or oblivious to our private conversation.

Odessa gives me a 'so what?' shrug.

How dare she!

I get the picture.

Odessa was protecting her good side because her mother was crouched on the love seat checking me out! The old spy is still sitting up, erect, thin and black as a fireplace poker.

I cannot excuse this insult.

"Sorry, Bub." Odessa finally says. "She really was sleeping."

That's not good enough.

I throw my hands up and lean into the space between Odessa and me with a frown of disbelief.

Her mother is a drunk. Therefore a thief.

"*Pozhaluista*!"

A cursing thief. What the hell is she saying?

"She's my *mother*." Odessa says it with such soft harshness that I suppose it should answer my objection.

It doesn't. It only answers why Odessa has to leave Marco with Cicero and me.

You don't leave your kid with a drunk, even if she does paint real well by the Black Sea.

"Bub, come over here," Odessa says.

I don't move. I can't believe Madame spy was here the whole time.

"Bub, I'm not going to infect you."

That's a cheap shot. I gave Odessa too much credit before about having the soul of a saint.

Fine. I walk up to her right side, just to

show her that I'm not any more afraid of being infected than she is of her scarface.

I see something blue on her toes as she wiggles them.

Ha! I see what those are. They say B-E-A-T-N-A-V-Y-!-! in blue nail polish. The Army-Navy football game is tonight. "Did Marco see that?"

"No, he's going to the game with Stubie."

"*Neuzheli.*"

"Be polite, mom," Odessa says. "Speak English."

"What did she say?" I ask.

"Indeed."

I look over my shoulder and see Madame staring back at me, as if she knows something.

She doesn't know anything. Except the price of vodka.

"I want to ask you something," Odessa says.

"I need to ask you something," I tell her. Her eyes are more insistent.

"I want you to be Marco's father."

The words fill me with a heartwarming fullness. "Cicero would be overjoyed," I tell her. "And me. I would be, too."

"I want you to convert to Catholicism."

"What — to make sure Marco grows up Catholic, you mean?"

"No, Stubie will do that. He's godfather. When you're ready, you'll take over."

"I'll tell you right now I'm not joining a church that worships Mary."

"Do you reject Marco if you honor me?"

"What?"

I look over my shoulder because I feel Madame's red eyes on me. Someone give that old woman a bottle so she can *do* something with herself.

"Bub?"

"What."

"Think about that. I'm not forcing you. I'm inviting you. This is my dying invitation. I know you read the Bible."

"Of course."

"You'll read your way right into the church."

"On one condition," I tell her.

"No conditions."

"Marco gets my name."

"No. He's my boy. It stays Cruz."

The thought occurs to me that this is more Odessa's meeting with me than my meeting with Odessa. How did that happen?

"There's something else I want to tell you, Bub, but not now." Odessa looks away to the door. "Smell that?"

I smell it. Pepper and onion. Dinner. It means I have to go.

"What was your question?" She reaches across her sunken hips with her left arm just far enough to hold my finger tips.

The blood-warm touch makes me lose confidence in my question, making it seem accusatory. But I look at her, already committed to ask it, my good eye to her good eye.

"How do you know you are going to die?" She pulls her hand back.

"How do you know you love Cicero?"

The novice brings Odessa a glass of brown brew with a straw, which Odessa takes with her left hand.

I thought she pulled her hand away from

me because she was offended by my question.

I don't answer her question about Cicero because it's rhetorical.

"It's sublime, right?" She draws a sip. "You're the writer. Don't things sometimes go beyond words?"

Again with the rhetorical question.

"It's one of those things." The tea browns her teeth. "You just know."

"You answered my question with a question," I tell her.

"The answer wouldn't make sense to you."

"Let me judge. Just to inspire confidence."

"Okay. Take this."

I take her tea, which smells like soil, and I hand her a Saint Gemma holy card that hasn't been laminated so she can write something on it.

Then she seals it in a mini envelope, and puts a tau cross on it. I trade her the tea for the envelope.

"After I'm dead," she says. "Read the answer."

"You mean I have to wait that long?"

"It won't be long. So you better tell me."

"Tell you what?"

"What you came to tell me."

"Oh, God! My ninth step. I have to ask you to forgive me."

"I do." She's beaming with brown teeth and a stroke-smile.

"Not yet." I tell her, holding back my own smile. "You have to wait until I tell you everything."

"Okay, then, I don't forgive you."

"Good."

Book Three

EXPOSURE

The Sweetness of Mourning

This hymn will wreck me the next time the refrain comes around, and if I'm going to get through this funeral with dry eyes for Marco's sake, I need to detach myself from its milk-and-honey melody.

I was doing fine until a moment ago, holding Marco while this liturgy came alive with the processional hymn. But I was swept into the harmony of the inclining notes that broke in the heights and dropped me on a plateau of unexpected exposure. My undoing was in the words:

"And he will raise you up on eagle's wings
Bear you on the breath of dawn
Make you to shine like the sun

And hold you in the palm of his hand."

The words run ruin through me, so that nothing's left in my heart that isn't limp. When I divert myself to consider how I have soared on the wings of absolution for two weeks since I did my ninth step with Odessa, the Poor Clares in their aisle-facing choir stalls propel us toward that refrain again.

I can't sing it without losing it, but if I taper my voice to a whisper, so that only my lips move, I'll keep control. And no one will see what a mess I am in the face of grace.

Odessa wanted her funeral here, in this old A-frame chapel, and not in the sanctuary with the gold dome overlooking the river, because this is where she prayed.

The pews and banisters are dark with hard varnished shells, and the thin alcove windows seem to trap as much light in the color-frost saints as they let through. The statues are doll-size, the beam work is common like barn framing, and the altar is ignoble, with fourteen thin Roman-style columns supporting the white marble table. There is a plain ivory tabernacle atop it, and a banner with red tassels that says 'Jesus Saves.'

The accouterments are almost childlike.

And now it grabs me how wrong I am. About everything, as usual.

I feel the expansion of Marco's side ribs into my chest as he inhales, and I notice how balanced he is in my hold as the priest kisses the altar. Marco is at ease.

Odessa wanted the funeral here because this is where *he* came.

He climbed under the altar and raced his cars up the aisle. *He* lay on his back and looked at the apse painted heaven-blue with gold stars, while his mother's lips moved quietly in the first pew. It's for him that we're all here.

And in spite of the strain that holding Marco puts on my back, which has gotten worse with the cold weather, nothing feels more natural or certain than to have him in my arms.

As unlikely as it sounds to hear myself say it, Marco is no longer a knot but a tie between Cicero and me.

I look to my left and see that Cicero's hair is as long as it's been in two years – I noticed it right away when she moved back in with Marco, but today I realize how much growth she's allowed it – enough to tie a small rabbit tail in back with a black satin bow. Her hair is gold with strawberry blush in the uneven light of the hanging lanterns.

It's the first time she's stood next to me in a church since we were married.

Cicero and Marco moved back into High Street two days after I visited Odessa.

I was the one who called Cicero the morning after I confessed to Odessa and asked Cicero to come home, but Emily Cruz had already worked out the arrangement that made it possible for Cicero to accept.

The arrangement was that Cicero and I wouldn't speak anything about my affair with Odessa unless we both agreed on a date to do it at least four days in advance – a classic Emily Cruz gimmick – but so far we haven't set that date.

We've been too busy moving Marco's furniture out of the infirmary, and putting up the

Christmas lights, and getting the pantry ready for the baby with the crib and the diaper gear and the twist-key musical bunny mobile we play to get Marco in the mood for a little sister.

In the two weeks since she's been back, Cissy and I have talked more about our future, and less about how I can make more money or when she's going to defend her Ph.D. thesis, than any time since we moved up from the city.

All she cares about is that I'm going to be there.

I'm going to be there.

A father's duty is to protect; provision comes second.

And a man who abandons his family in the service of a superior income is worse than the deadbeat dad who at least is honest with the world that he doesn't live a shit for his wife and kids.

I should know. It's all I've been thinking about since Marco's been back.

On Friday, I went with Marco to get Odessa's dying instructions, and on Saturday, while Marco was on stage for his Christmas play, Odessa died.

Cicero and I both thought we should have pulled Marco out of the play and gotten him to the infirmary, because we knew Odessa was dying as early as that afternoon, but Odessa insisted that Marco stay in the play to deliver his angel Gabriel line — Odessa's own favorite line — "Be not afraid." That's the way Odessa wanted to remember him.

But Cicero and I should have overruled her. It wasn't right to take Marco to the empty room, his mommy's body gone from the bed, his furniture neat and alone by the window with his Christmas presents at the fireplace.

He wailed more because he couldn't find her than anything else.

Odessa had told him that when she died, her body would stay behind like a puddle after rain that you aren't supposed to splash in, but that her life would be alive like water in the river on its way to the ocean. Marco wanted to see what that looked like, and there was no consoling him.

Cicero thought the problem was that Marco never got a chance to say good bye, but that wasn't the problem.

Marco's been saying good bye to Odessa for a year. And Odessa to him.

Odessa fitted Marco for his little black suit for this day when she said he would be the guest of honor at her Welcome Home Mass, and she gave him a little brass decanter of lavender oil that she said he could open as many times as he needed to feel her hug.

Odessa was big on lavender oil. She told me Friday to keep that jar full.

I'm going to dilute the thing as soon as we get home. I'm already sick of the smell of it.

It suddenly perplexes me, as the priest makes small cross marks on his forehead, lips and heart, that this whole tragedy with Cicero and the underwear and the separation and Dickens could have been avoided had I only stuck to my resolution at Goloborza to do no harm, denied Cicero's suspicion, and allowed Odessa to die with our secret.

It could have all been avoided, and yet had events followed my design, I would never be in the place I am now, holding Marco as my own; being united with Cicero; standing in the same pew as Brutus Cruz, unable to keep my eyes from tearing at the name of a gracious God who no one has ever seen.

I can't explain it. I can only accept it that the heart wrench I suffered for three months after Cicero left worked out better than my best plan to avoid it.

There was something about those iced nights of separation on High Street that surpassed the cups of my top nights drunk. Origen calls that counterintuitive. I call it grace, because the best booze I ever used was never a toast to the things I revered or trusted or knew.

From the time my old man got busted until a year ago when I fell into the program, nothing made sense, nothing was sacred, nothing that looked worthwhile ever proved true.

I was a killer who knew it. And the booze that took my mind off that fact was too precious to question.

What I don't understand is how Origen winds up hardhearted and childless for never wanting the abortions, yet I who wanted my son dead from the beginning get to hold him with a love that transcends my own nature. The only explanation is God. Only by the supernatural do I protect what's mine.

If Marco had not lived, there would be nothing left of me for Cicero to want, nothing in life for Odessa to love, nothing worth second vows for Brutus and Emily Cruz, and certainly no reason for Madame to leave the Black Sea. I would be like Origen. A man without a home. A killer with the world to roam.

A burst of guttural sobs comes from Odessa's mother, the Madame-in-mourning, sitting in an altar server's chair outside the sacristy.

She refused to be seated in the pews.

Her hair is wind-thrown, her eyes are sunken, and her lips are bleached of color.

But in the coffin, Odessa sparkles with her good side in profile, her scars buried in the white silk pillow, and her face toward the altar.

Even now, after everything, she goes out gorgeous. I'm sure she left Madame in charge of the post-mortem details, right down to the hair curl above Odessa's jeweled left ear.

I try not to think about the emotion that's driving Madame's tears, not for my sake, but for Marco's. If I think too much, I might connect, and when I connect, I cry.

What is this pleasure I take in sorrow for someone I never knew except in the way I reduced her, someone I admired too late, who I will never cry for again?

I take my sobriety so religiously, and yet I am overcome by this insincere grief, this shallow show of lukewarm tears.

If Marco is looking to me for an authentic reaction, he would be better off watching Brutus, who was here early on his knees when the rest of us came in, his shoulders like side tables in his square blue suit, and his black-and-white hair cut to bristles. He has been statue-stoic all afternoon, but with one remarkable change: he's wearing a red AIDS solidarity ribbon on his lapel.

You couldn't have even mentioned the word

to him before today.

I'm sure the ribbon was an Odessa instruction to him before she died. I have no doubt she hit him up for more than that, too.

When I took Marco to see her and sign papers Friday night, Odessa had no scruples about trying to arrange more control after her death than she ever had in life.

She made me read a letter at her bedside about the pecking order of adults in Marco's rearing on matters of faith, morals, school, arts and sports. I ranked second below Brutus in all five categories. The letter also said that I should never make a decision of consequence about Marco without praying on it for an hour in front of the tabernacle in a Catholic church.

The pecking order and the holy hour are both problems, of course, but I didn't tell her that because I was reading the most difficult condition: never tell Marco about the abortion set on him.

There was nothing sinister about me standing there nodding and finally saying 'Yes,' when Odessa asked me to agree — and made me look at her when I said it — because she wouldn't have died in peace if I hadn't.

I suspect Odessa was playing me off Brutus for Marco's benefit anyway, because she told me again, like I would ever forget it, "I gotta warn you, Bub, Stubie thinks you're scared of him."

We stand for The Lord's Prayer but I don't hold Marco, because Cicero is thinking about not standing.

I know the girl is pregnant, and all this rising and kneeling is hard for her, but I think Cicero can manage for this occasion, and I give her help on the elbow that says as much. She glances me off but stands.

Odessa wrote Cicero a letter, too. Cicero read it but would only tell me afterwards: "O.D. is no saint."

I wonder whether Odessa would qualify for sainthood on dying a good death alone. On Friday, she had taken down her holy cards and put them on a key ring for Marco.

Marco knows the story behind each saint and cherished the present at first. Then he got disturbed that the cards were out of place. It was a conflicting moment for the guy; but he kept the cards.

Odessa gave me the hatbox with the tapes for Marco, color-coded with red, yellow and green dots to match my master list: green for anytime, yellow for holidays, and red restricted.

The green titles ring from the same theme: 'How Much Mommy Loves You,' 'Why You Are Mommy's Precious Gift' and 'God Loves You So Much.'

The red ones have the provocative titles like 'Why You Notice Girls' and 'When Your Father Comes to You.'

I learned on Friday night that Odessa told Marco his real Daddy had been living near Marco since he was born, and the Daddy made Odessa promise not to tell Marco who he was because he didn't think he was a good enough Daddy. Odessa told Marco that she agreed to keep the Daddy's secret only because the Daddy was trying to become better, and when he got better the first thing the Daddy promised to do was come to live with Marco and take care of him after Odessa died.

Odessa told Marco she had been angry at the Daddy for a long time but she forgave him, and Marco should forgive him, too.

Looking down at Marco on the kneeler, his chin barely clearing the pew rail, and his eyes intent on the priest sanctifying the bread and wine, I wonder how many of Odessa's tapes talk about religious vocation.

She also gave me seven letters for Marco to unseal on milestones like the first anniversary of her death, the eve of his first Communion, and one that I will definitely read first called 'When Your Dad Starts Catechism.'

I stay back with Marco in the pew during Communion, thinking I can console him, but a nun singing "I Am The Bread of Life" a cappella hits a C note so high during the refrain, '*I will raise you up*,' that I lose grip on the turmoil inside me and the mess tears out before I can cover my face.

I think I feel even Brutus' hand on my back, patting it to console me.

It's better to let it all out this way — all of this regret that churns with shame and defeat, because once it is spent and cool on the outside, it can no longer disgrace you.

I feel new hands on my arm and shoulder, hands more sure to the touch. Nuns hands, I imagine.

If the nuns knew I was crying for myself, they would be less sympathetic.

But who says they don't know? No one cries this way for someone else.

Only despair cries this way. Despair that you have known God too late to have the life he offered you before you went your own way.

Yet God has given me everything.

He took everything away, and before he gave it back, he ordered it according to all that vexed me, so that I wouldn't lose it again, so that not a single thing that he has given me will be lost.

Emily Cruz is rubbing my back with an unsteady touch, as though she worries I may brush it off. I owe her a ninth step amends, which I'll arrange after I confess to Cicero tomorrow night.

But there is no time to think of that now. We are standing again.

I reach down to pick up Marco. Brutus Cruz and Madame yielded to my insistence last night that no one should delay the Benediction and get up to speak about Odessa in the past tense in front of Marco, so I have to hold up my end of the agreement to bring Marco to view the casket.

I don't know how to do it.

Cicero is the first one out of the pew, but she won't lead by example. Just as I thought, she stops in the aisle to let me go first, carrying Marco, to approach Odessa's still, perfect profile.

It's as though the church has cleared out, as though the space between the casket and my new black wingtips is shorter than my own breath.

The thought comes to me that Odessa used to have great lines. She could stop you in mid-stride and make you ask her to say it again.

She never would.

I think that's because she had only one line.

I can't remember what it was.

I need a line right now. We are both just standing here over her, son and man.

Odessa's left shoulder, dressed in a

shimmering pink bishop's sleeve, is propped higher than the other, so that her neck lies flat and her pose seems natural, with her olivewood Rosary beads in hand. And a glass feather on the pillow.

Wait a minute. What *is* that? It's a crystal-like sparrow feather, pliable and glossy with life.

The feather of an angel.

It's only there in my imagination, I'm sure of it, but instantly I know what to say to Marco: "Her angel is here if you want to tell her something."

Marco looks at me with raised eyebrows as though what I said makes sense. Then a deep frown comes across his eyes and sits on his lips. Leaning into the casket he says: "I don't like Christmas."

Outside, it is snowing again, and I keep the radio off during the ride home with Cicero and Marco. The only music in Cicero's car is Christmas music.

There is no escaping the fact that Christmas is coming — tomorrow is Christmas Eve — and Marco got me thinking how hard it will be to tear into the presents only a few days into mourning. It was Marco's choice whether or not to attend the burial, and he said no; my choice whether or not to show up at the reception and I said no way.

At home, I get Marco out of the back seat, but I don't follow Cicero into the kitchen. Marco is in no hurry to go inside.

Snowflakes as fat as popcorn fall on the porch steps.

"We didn't watch the snow," Marco says.

"You don't watch the snow," I tell him. "You shovel it."

"We watched the rain and the leaves."

"I don't have a good answer for you." It feels as though every word I need to make a damn sentence is the weight of a truck tire. "When it snows you don't watch it. You shovel it before it buries you."

I wish I hadn't said that.

Now he's going to think about Odessa being buried by the snow.

I can't think how to get his mind off of it.

The light in the gray sky is leaving.

Soon it will be dark. And it dawns on me what to tell him. The angel who left the feather on the pillow must be following me.

"I have a mystery for you," I tell him.

"What?"

"Do you know what a mystery is?"

"Something sad."

"Something we believe because God said it."

Marco follows me inside and I put him on his bed. I turn off the wall lamp near the alcove where we have his stuff from the infirmary, and I take off his black shoes so that he can lie down.

From the advent wreath I pull out the candle that we haven't lit yet and empty the peppermints from a glass dish to use as the base.

"Let's see." I light the white candle and turn its top wax against the flame to make melt in the dish bottom for the candle to stand.

"See what?" He says.

"See if Jesus is right."

I get onto the bed with him and lay down my head next to his.

"The light shines in the darkness and the darkness cannot overtake it."

The Two Wills

Cicero wants to know why I made this mess.

The woman has protested since noon that I was making too much food — that she didn't need stuffed duck this year — and that she didn't want to spend our big night watching me work the kitchen.

Her protests I thought were a courtesy. Cicero loves stuffed duck. And if a cook doesn't cook for Christmas Eve, when does he cook?

But Brutus and Emily Cruz have already taken Marco to midnight Mass, and as I chip the char off the broiler pan, the reality sets that I still have an hour or more of breakdown to do that truthfully cannot wait until morning.

I have more work to do than Cicero has patience, and I suppose it could look like I'm dragging on my ninth step with her.

The fact is this activity has more to do with my thrashing around last night than it does with any plan to procrastinate, because I was harassed until dawn with Odessa's last words on the Saint Gemma card: "No appetite."

I woke up determined to be hungry.

But when I turn to Cicero to tell her that, she's sitting cross-legged and agitated, tapping her fingers on the kitchen table, bloated in the throat and red in the cheeks from the citrus sauce.

She's no longer in shape to undress in front of me to get what she wants.

In an instant, my mind recalls the bed sheets last night, when I could sense with my hand on the mattress that Cicero wanted to be laid, the same way you feel with your foot on the floor of the car the lay of the road.

I haven't understood her that way before, and I should be grateful for it, other things being the same.

But they're not.

Cicero clears the sheets of old bedware now, and she is no longer driven by underwear that shouts, but maternity briefs and clean brassieres.

And although I found a way to excite our old positions by shaking the bed during penetration, so that I was surprised last night to taste a bit of spit that glanced her lip when I stretched up to kiss her, the act of sideways intercourse behind the smoothed-tight banks of her stomach is still more circumspect than erotic.

"What's the matter?" Cicero looks at me in a pained way, as though she read my thought.

I feel naked without my patch.

Cicero gave my prosthesis back to me when she moved in. It was still in the Parisienne.

"You know what this is? All of this?" I wave

my towel through the kitchen air. “Know what Odessa’s note said?”

“Which one?”

I give the holy card to Cicero to read.

“I asked her how she knew she was dying,” I tell Cissy.

“I can’t believe you asked her that.”

“And all last night I was thrashing, thinking I’d lost my appetite.”

“So you had to prove you had one? That’s funny, baby. But this is too much. You have to leave it. Or I’m going to sleep on you.”

“Look at this kitchen.”

“Maybe you should go to C.I.A.”

“Two years and twenty-thousand, I don’t think so.” She’s talking about the Culinary Institute of America. “I’d rather find a partner and buy The Tabard.”

“I meant tell you,” she says. “He got reviewed in the Times.”

“Who did.”

“Alastair Barnes. I think they gave him a ‘very good.’”

“The New York Times would never give Barnes a ‘very good.’”

Cicero slides off the chair to the kitchen carpet. She pirouettes on her knees in black stretch leggings that you would expect to see on the white wine women at Paco’s, and she crawls to the Christmas tree in the corner, where my baker’s rack was.

The rounds of her bottom have kept their definition.

Her apricot hair glances a bough as she lifts her left thigh off the rug. She braces her arms in thin black sleeves behind her, bouncing the ankle of her white bare foot the way she does when she knows she has you.

"I want my present."

She thinks her ninth step is going to be exciting to behold. It isn't.

What little I have that hasn't already slipped out in our fights is not going to impress her, and we've got that four-day rule about discussing Odessa still in effect.

As I start to tell her, I feel myself peeling back from my own confession. It feels scripted. The words don't hold the weight they should, even though the words are sincere, even though they are mine.

A thought drops to mind that Jared of the Sorrows was right when he told me to stop reading to him.

I was reading my wrongs from my fourth step list of resentments to Jared when the Sorrows told me, "Let's use this step to learn how to talk to each other." I thought we *were* talking to each other. I had been reading off my offenses against the people on my 84-person resentment list, and at the time, I was sure that Jared stopped me because *he* wanted to do all the talking.

But maybe I understand his point, if his point was that one truth from the heart beats all the facts in the head.

I drop my ninth step notes on the kitchen table and sit in the rocking chair, near the young tree, close enough to Cicero that our feet could touch.

"Look, I wrote it down because I was afraid I'd forget something if I didn't, but there's nothing really horrible that we haven't talked about."

I smell her perspiration.

"The thing is as I was writing it, I felt a detachment. A separation, you know? I don't blame you for this stuff like I used to. I don't blame God. I don't put myself in prison for it, you know?"

"No."

"What?"

"I don't know, baby."

I'm telling her all the crime I pulled with the extra cash register and the dope at the Porticoes and the finger circles with the Seventh Avenue girls doesn't sate my appetite anymore.

I used to steal and get docked for stealing but still love the thief life. I used to drink to my ruin but honor the high times. I dealt Thai stick and played seat fingers with the three o'clock girls and went to jail for 90 days because one of them with the spirit of Potiphar's wife set me up with possession, but I scolded the voices of correction that blamed my trouble on addiction.

I loved the shit I pulled.

And my mother in one of her letters was right — my own error was my God.

"What I did I don't love anymore," I tell Cissy. "You don't get that?"

"I'm waiting for details. I don't mind if you read that thing."

"I thought it would be better if we talked."

"We'll talk when I know what you did."

"You know what I did. I ran porno scripts in my head every day."

"That's supposed to make me feel better?"

"I'm telling you it doesn't own me anymore."

"And I'm supposed to believe you?"

"What choice do you have? I can't prove it. It's like drinking. The only thing between me and my next drink is God. I never had that before. The porno is the same way."

"You want me to believe that all these fantasies you have for other women are over because you *have* God?"

"I'm telling you I'm separated from it — I don't *have* to go to it."

I notice she stopped dangling her white ankle. It's twitching.

"This is supposed to be my ninth step," she says.

"This is *my* step. I have to get sober. We can argue until Epiphany, but if you want your present, you gotta trust me. There are no guarantees for tomorrow. There is only today and what I'm doing today."

Cicero is quiet, and that's a problem.

If she stays silent too long, she hardens.

The other thing is this *is* supposed to be her step, and I just shut her out of it.

I'm going back to my script.

"I'm sorry. I reach up to grab my paper. "You're right."

She props her knees apart. Her distended belly slopes between her thighs to a smaller conical hood under her stretched tights that obscures the convex I'm used to seeing there, and I wonder if I really know this woman with the new shape, hearing my confession.

I read to her: "I used the fact that you had a good-paying job as an excuse not to go out and get better work."

"See, baby, I never cared about that — "

"...You wanted to have a baby when we moved to the city, but I didn't care. I turned you into my problem. I made you my unhappiness. I was never secure. I didn't have my own answers. Nothing fulfilled me. I blamed you for that."

"Baby, you had answers."

"Those weren't answers."

"I don't know what you expect."

"Don't ever think I had answers."

In my mind's eye Charlie Gul comes walking through the Porticoes the night of my 21st birthday when I didn't suspect him or think to guard my mouth, and I told him that I had been with Odessa.

"You liberated her," the liar told me. But I was the liar because I believed him. I didn't believe him because I thought it was true. I believed him because I thought it was new.

"You know what it was?" I tell her. "My own error was my god."

"Who said that? Your mother?"

God, I hate it when Cicero suspects me.

Why couldn't she trust me to make the connection myself?

The problem is she doesn't think I'm serious.

"My mother? My mother doesn't make connections. It's Augustine's quote anyway. And I had to admit it."

Cissy is picking tinsel off the carpet; either she doesn't care about my point, or she's acting like she doesn't care.

I'm tempted to press it, but something tells me to leave it, because this last item in my ninth step notes is more important. To make it stick, I have to dunk my pride lower than it is now.

Suddenly I sense in the focus of Cissy's eyes that she's going to confront me with something.

"Why did you do it? Cicero says it from the same distance that she had with the underwear in her fist in August.

"I thought we agreed to set a date if we were going to talk about that."

"What do you think I'm talking about?"

She's talking about Odessa. If she says she's not, she's lying.

"I mean the train, baby."

"Yeah, the train."

"I would have picked you up — why didn't you call?"

"I didn't go out to kill myself."

"How could you walk home after that? I would have come right away. I had to hear it from the police. They didn't know where you were. Why didn't you call me?"

"What was there to say?"

"What is there to say now?"

She's got good questions.

It's not that she doesn't have good questions.

But answers are always better, even if they're not always at my service.

Everything has changed since Dickens.

I got back into AA. Origen confessed. The sun danced. I confessed. My kid came home. And now Cissy is back.

I've been in places words don't go.

I go back to my ninth step notes.

Thank God for the notes.

"Listen to me — I watched you beat the street cheat...remember in the Village? And I thought you were a genius. When you wore your hat with the Charlie Brown flaps at the Lincoln Center thing — I remember thinking you were like, above fashion."

As I tell her, her mouth is tight, because she doesn't know where I'm going. I'm talking about how she exposed a Washington Square Park Rastafarian who wanted to sell me an $80-dollar bag of glued up oregano, and how she shamed a Broadway scam artist by laughing off his fake money roll that he wanted to switch-and-run on me.

But I also think back to Bethlehem, when she grabbed the truck driver's jeans and got chased getting away in her Mustang.

Her luck was better than her smarts.

I picture Cicero on Stone's dentist chair, lapping up his vibrator rap, and it occurs to me that smarts only go as far as the will allows.

Cicero looks perplexed.

"I would see the good things about you through a magnifying glass as though I alone had discovered them, but on the booze you looked insecure to me and overeducated and, you know, prudish — "

"Prudish?"

"That's how I saw you — not how you are."

"That makes me feel much better."

"Cissy — I was a spy. I used my inside knowledge against you to hurt you and blame you. I turned you into my opponent, because I knew how to beat you. And that magnifying glass blew up everything that was weak about you. It wasn't love. It was wrong."

"That's too good." She's shaking her head and smirking.

"What is?"

"To come from you. The magnifying glass. Where did you get it?"

"It came out of my mouth, didn't it?"

Okay, I got it out of the AA Big Book, but I had to *find* it. I had to make the connection.

It's not some plug-in formula like her secular psychology models.

"Why can't you give me credit for trying to change?" I tell her. "What about..."

"What?"

I look for my towel to finish cleaning.

"Go ahead say it."

For Cicero to disperse my confession because I didn't come up with some of these insights myself is complete deceit, because *she* says nothing about the human condition that she can't square with Freud.

I wasn't going to mention it, because she's got to bear her own error, but I translated her six Latin words in the frame. They mean *A happy life is a tranquil mind.*

"A happy life is a tranquil mind," I say. "Whose bad motto is that?"

"Where did you get that?" She wants to shoot up in wrath, but her stomach won't allow it. "Did you take it? It was my father's."

"You had it in your drawer."

"It was my father's!"

I didn't expect it to be her father's.

Her father was a Virgil scholar who didn't publish, and switched to selling real estate.

And when profession and possession didn't fill the hole, he turned to digression. With a former college student. On a boat. A propane explosion. And a fire that burned to the waterline.

I can't stand people who preach peace, peace, peace.

You can't have peace once without justice.

"Why are you so hostile to anything that didn't hang on a cross?" Cicero says. "Christ didn't use psychology?"

"Christ used forgiveness."

"What are you accusing me of? Do you even know?"

"If psychology could do the job, wouldn't it have done it already?"

"Where has religion done better, except where it has done worse?"

"The point is a happy death, not a happy life."

That stops her.

And it stops me, too, because I'm not sure where I got it.

Then another thought arrives: *You can't make her believe you.*

It's confusing, because I've always thought that if you share the Gospel with enough skill and conviction, it's a forgone conversion.

As I sit with my arms folded, looking into the winter black of Christmas Eve out the kitchen window, I wonder which side to take — my own or the one going against me.

Picture-thoughts of Origen drop into my blind sight. I see Ori's shark skin head and pink poncho wings. I see him icing his balls before the big cut, standing on the Golden Gate Bridge as a testament to all the untouchables with bad fathers and no futures.

It strikes me that Ori has acted on his own worst impulses without swallowing a gram of my Christian counsel. Yet my own faith in God didn't die because it failed to change Origen.

I confessed to Odessa, for crying out loud. Marco is my own now.

I've received my life back.

I don't go back to cleaning, but I take a seat on the carpet a foot away from my wife. Cicero thinks

Origen is a fraud who doesn't accrue anything. She thinks I've given him every credit he has, and that no one but a sucker should care what he believes, because he makes it up as he goes along.

Of course, she could be partly right. It's a huge relief to admit it.

My own beliefs are no secret, nor are Cicero's, but if I had to write down Origen's manifesto, I could never pick up the pen, because I would never be able to put it down.

He clouds the Buddha with Lenape smoke, he knifes the Bhagavad Gita with the horns of Gnosticism, and he defiles the great monotheistic religions with his catchall New Age poetry: *the sacred scrolls are bare, but if you want some with writing on them, we can find those, too.*

And I realize that Origen has done to me what his father the biochemist did to him.

His father staked out his own no-trespass territory where Ori couldn't duel him. So the son followed: Origen retreats to the maze when someone tries to reach his religion. It's a survival act.

When someone gets close, Origen gets lost.

It's interesting how I prayed on the holy mountain for one connection and didn't get it. And now without asking I have more answers than I can connect.

I marvel at how Cicero's bloated belly and bigger breasts inspire my desire, and it occurs to me that the source of Cicero's attraction is coming from behind the scene, where her heart is budding with new life.

"You're right," I have to nudge her heel to get a response.

"That's twice tonight."

"I'm sorry." Now I'm the one picking up tinsel. "I'm not supposed to bring you into this. I'm supposed to sweep my side of the street and that's it."

"You've promised me all these wonderful revelations."

"You have all that I have."

"It doesn't feel like mine."

"If you're expecting me to square a thesis in front of you, I'll tell you what — nothing's new under the sun. I got the magnifying glass from the Big Book if you want to know, but it's still exactly how I felt."

"And what about now?"

Another impossible Cicero question.

I search the universe for an answer.

Any answer.

But it doesn't come.

Until I remember to do what Cissy does when she's on the hook, and I change the subject.

"Look at you," I tell her.

Cicero glances down and strokes her stomach. She's pleased by my answer, which gives me another idea.

"All things are new." I smile.

"God, another Bible verse?"

"Is it?" Let's see if she knows whether it is or not. I'll bet she doesn't.

Cicero smiles again, looking at her belly with expectation — the same anticipation that lifted Marco's face when we told him that he could open Odessa's present before dinner.

I fight the prompt in my mind that calls my thoughts to that bad scene earlier today with Marco, because I finally have Cicero feeling good about herself and looking great smiling, but I can't resist the summons to remember the little guy's anguish.

He tore into the purple tissue paper and saw the red leather Bible Odessa had annotated for him.

Odessa had graced the pages with color caricatures and commentaries and dime-sized cut-out photographs of their vacations and birthdays. She showed me five fantastic pages in Genesis briefly while Marco was in the bathroom the last night we saw her.

But when he opened the Bible this afternoon, he frowned and threw it against the kitchen window.

Nothing broke. And he limped away.

"Baby? Is it another quote?"

"I'm looking at the Christmas pudding. It has turned blueberry-gray and probably has twice the flavor now that it's cool.

I hook the bowl with my index finger and drag it across the table toward Cicero, but when she sees it coming she makes a blowfish face with her cheeks.

She showed me that face the first night in Bethlehem. It means she wants to be laid.

For the first time tonight, I have the advantage; all things being new as they are.

I could tell Cissy that it is from the mouth of Christ, or I could tell her it's from my mouth to hers.

"It's the truth," I tell her. "I mean, look at you."

One Nature

Horses with nostrils in clouds of steam bite the white-frosted grass across the street, and two deer with winter hide as dark as a lion's underbeard freeze in the shade at the ridge of the woods, waiting for our car to pass. Downhill at the outlet, there's a glistening on the cattails, and a mist lifting off the glass-black reservoir. I could point out these things to Marco in the back seat, ostensibly to get him thinking about something other than Odessa's tapes, or to Cicero to get her mind off the due date, but I wonder whether I'm just a sucker for the sentimental who sees too much connection in what's common.

Phyllis Stein would have me think so.

She fooled me into believing she was serious when she clapped her hands and called me into her office to praise my piece about the Hudson River School oil exhibition in the Carthage museum.

Wicked tit.

There was nothing wrong with my piece.

I knew something was up when I saw Phyllis Stein's red-rimmed grin, and then the orange-lump spill on a printout of my story. An old bulimic's trick. She was beside herself with glee as I stood there stunned.

"Good as far as I got sick on it!" She said. "Resend it!"

Of course I had to move some words around, but I saved the original and read it again at home. One or maybe two phrases were over the top. The rest of the story was *fine*. Only a nihilist like Phyllis Stein would object. The Hudson River School painters were romantics. That's the point. If a factory or a rail spur was in the landscape, they would leave it off the canvass. They painted only what they *saw*.

The moon-white glow of the late January sun makes the morning seem dreamy.

The time travel won't last.

At high speed on Route 12, I see the upright oval breast of a falcon perched in a bare hardwood. The puffed-up chest reminds me of Brutus Cruz, waiting for me at West Point, and I don't want to be reminded of Brutus Cruz waiting for me at West Point.

We'll be there soon enough, although I haven't figured how to tell Cicero that I'm wrestling him this morning. She warned me not to do it.

I'll take Route 12 to the Hudson River, then Old Broadway up to the Bear Mountain Bridge, where we'll cross the river and be at West Point by 10 a.m.

The Madame wants to see Marco before she goes back to the Black Sea. She's actually going to Turkey, where the women of her family have lived since 1918. A place called Bafra. Educated people have never heard of it. Marco had to show it to me on a map.

Cicero isn't any crazier about showing up for the Madame's adieu than Emily or Brutus or me.

At the Hudson River, snow-crusted ice patches stretch like amoebae islands in both directions.

They look like Holstein spots, only inverted, with the field black and the pattern white.

I don't see how you can look at something so naturally spectacular like that and not be moved with wonder.

If my old man Adamo Dante taught me anything, it was to give nature its due.

That and to change with the season. "Whether you're ready or not," he would say with a grin. "It's change or die. You can't survive out of season."

The irony is that little motto is a major league AA coupon — not the one about surviving out of season, but the one about changing or dying.

My old man was talking about chanterelles and Cuban melons and winter citrus. That's all he meant by change. Cicero likes to give him credit for meaning more, but she does that a lot with him. She did it again last night.

But if my old man meant more than cooking with what's in season, he was no genius for it, because wisdom never says run like hell *away* from change. That cat moved in *mid*-season he feared change so much.

Cicero asked me last night why I was angry with him, as though she didn't know. As though the post card he sent is innocent. He wants me to come to Brussels where he has a new partner and a new restaurant. What he really wants is his recipes. But he hasn't the guts to ask for them because his shame as a bad father has always overshadowed his actions.

It doesn't matter about the damn recipes. I threw them out with my other articles of misplaced faith in September.

"He's a thief," I told her when she asked. "All drunks are thieves."

She thought she had me when she said "So your amends are only good for the good people."

She thought so because I didn't say anything back.

I didn't say anything back because I was thinking: *If that was true, I wouldn't have done one with you.*

I finally told her I didn't want to talk about it anymore.

And I don't.

The morning magic is ruined.

The points of undone things prick at my peace.

I'm soft prey for the annoying twitches of my uneasy wife, and the sullen stillness of my closet kid in the back.

Marco's got his headsets on every time I see him, wearing that same sunken look of withdrawal.

I know the end of January is Marco's funk time, and that somewhere in Marco's unconscious, if you listen to Ori, Marco's brain remembers the womb trauma of the abortion appointment.

But there's no way I can build up Marco by telling him how God worked it all out for good. Not with his mom dead less than a month. Not with Cicero next to me.

Cicero's fidgeting is winding me up. She can't get comfortable.

I don't know when she turned from expectant mom into discontented child carrier, but her conversion is complete.

She threatened to drink cod liver oil. I told her she could drive herself to the hospital if she did that. She wants the baby out. Hates to sit. And she twists back for the third time to get her hand on the seat knob to recline it.

"What are *those* doing in here?"

She can't possibly mean my old Dan Gables. I stuffed those wrestling shoes under the seat good.

"I saw those in the garage and I thought you were throwing them out."

In a moment she'll put it together.

I'm dead.

"So childish!" She hisses the words, snapping down the visor with the vanity mirror to check whether Marco noticed.

He's taking off his headsets.

The kid has first-born intuition. He can sense a fight before it's hot.

Good for me, because with Marco's eyes on the front seat, Cicero won't be able to spit blood. She'll can seethe all she wants with her brown boots on the dashboard, but to no effect. Let her cuss the silence. Threaten me by implication. It won't work.

Some things a man has to do he doesn't want to debate. Cicero doesn't understand that.

All the row and doubt you can summon in the service of making the "right" decision is as helpful to a man with a battle to win as the mockers who told Christ to get down from the cross.

There is no getting out of some things.

"You'll get hurt." Cicero says it with hope.

"I'm not going to get hurt. It's not a fight."

Cicero doesn't know what a real wrestling match is like.

She doesn't know because she doesn't want to know. She thinks wrestling is lowbrow Appalachia pay-per-view show business. I've never cared enough to define it until now.

"It's two points for a takedown, one point for an escape, three points for a near fall, and if you pin the guy, that's it. The match is over."

"You mean if he gives you a pin — "

"No. He's not going to give me anything. I'm going to *stick* him."

Cicero doesn't understand. I'm saying that I'm going to pin Brutus' middle-aged gonads and *stick* him in the first period.

"How are you going to do that?"

"I'm going to throw him."

"How many points do you get for that?"

"We'll see."

Marco is leaning forward to interrupt with some heavy Kindergarten inquiry that I know I don't have the patience to indulge, so I tell him:

"Wrestling is a friendly fight on a soft mat with a referee, except there won't be a referee today. Me and grandpa are just going to work out."

Cicero's clenched fists and straight-ahead-stare-at-nothing have as much to do with her own indecision about how far to fight me as they do any consideration of whether to expose Marco to a harsh car argument.

I wait until we stop at the foot of Bear Mountain to tell Cicero that I know how to beat Brutus, not because I'm stronger but because I'm smarter.

My bad knees and bad back and bad eye don't matter. I have the technique.

"He won't expect me to throw him."

Cicero wants to retort with some kind of ambush — I see it in the hunch of her shoulders — but she stops herself. Maybe she knows what I'll say.

Men are built to protect.

I've been daring her to tell me I'm wrong.

A man has to know what he believes.

He has to get control of his soul and defend what's his under God with fidelity and sacrifice. If Adam had done that, he wouldn't have needed to provide, because he would still be in the garden.

If my old man had done it, my mom might be in Brussels with him today.

If I had done it, Odessa would be alive, and I wouldn't be a pussy in a generation of pussies.

"Listen." I poke Cissy on the thigh as the beams of the Bear Mountain Bridge shift into the foreground. "Steuben thinks he can intimidate me because he's a bigger man. I'm not sinking to his level. I'm rising to his challenge, okay?"

"The Middle Ages are over."

"And men with it."

"Then why don't you take care of Charlie Gul?"

Cissy hates the fact that C-Gul opened a roadhouse in Banksville on the Greenwich border, fifteen minutes from our house.

She took a call from C-Gul on New Year's Eve and told him to go to hell.

She wants me to tell him the same thing.

"What do you mean 'take care of him?'" I mean, want does she think I can do? "C-Gul wants his money."

"I want him away from Marco and me. And you. For Good."

"I owe him seventy-two thousand dollars."

"Can he prove it?"

"He doesn't have to. I admit it."

"If you stole money from him..." Cicero is whispering, checking the vanity mirror. "He would have had you arrested, wouldn't he?"

"We were friends," I tell her.

"He didn't have you arrested because you didn't steal from him. He stole from you."

"This isn't about having proof on me. It's about having God on me. Being responsible and doing my amends."

"Do you want to go back to jail?"

"I don't want to go back to *hell*."

I'll bet she thinks I'm bluffing.

I'll teach her how wrong she is.

"I learned my lesson." I tell her. Marco is back to being completely somewhere else.

"In jail you did."

"At Golo I did. When I decided not to tell you about Odessa."

Now she knows I'm not bluffing.

"I'm not making that mistake again, if that's okay with you."

Being sober is about standing up to error and admitting your fault until there is nobody in the present who you can't look at eye to eye.

The extent that you fail to confess is the degree to which you stay locked in your own disdain.

The only way to freedom is to surrender the fight to be right.

I'm going to explain that to Cicero as soon as I can make it sound manlier.

Off the bridge, the army-green pines of West Point bend in the river wind, and the humid-sweet smell of Marco's lavender extract that I forgot to dilute keeps the present in the past, much as Cicero and I would like the moment to be in the future.

I don't prolong the greetings in the foyer at the Major and Mrs. Cruz's house, because it is only Emily Cruz who is here to meet us.

Brutus is waiting for me in the MacArthur gym.

He must have given Emily Cruz a stern debriefing about the wrestling match, because she hasn't complained.

She hasn't encouraged Cicero's hints of discontent either.

Madame apparently went on a walk, even though we were supposed to be here at 10 a.m., and here we are, on time.

I cross the hill toward the hospital, on a neat street with curled iron lanterns.

Snow from last week is still high on the curb.

A double set of cement steps where I've seen cadets take their outdoor classes leads to a subway-sized tunnel with the scores of Army-Navy games dating to 1939, and out the other end, past the old football stadium, I see the stunning bend of the river again.

There is something awesome about this fort town that bows at all turns to nature.

As I close in on the gym with its World War II-era hangar roof, the stark winterscape makes the brown MacArthur statue seem to contain every color in the spectrum.

The air is warm, damp and old inside the gym.

It's an impressive sky-high cave, tamed with lights and air-conditioning ducts.

I spot Brutus at the far end, stretching spread-eagle on a mat, while a dozen high-performance crewcut satellites run orbits around him on the track.

The burnt-orange ARMY letters high on the wall are fixed on pillars between five tower-shaped Venetian windows.

Brutus' legs are as black with hair as a bear's. His shoulders are like cannon mounts. And I have to say, without exaggeration, that his thick neck rotates about as nimbly as a turret on a tank.

I get a falling feeling in my stomach of a feat not sized up right.

Next is a searing thought that I've left myself no room to run.

Where's the coupon for panic? Oh yeah. *Move a muscle, change a thought.* I keep walking towards him. I tell myself that his 190 pounds is more burden than bulk.

Look at him. He's wearing new black Tigers and a red singlet.

A singlet is like the 1920s one-piece men's beach suit, except with deeper limb cuts. It's respectable enough for competition, but to suit up all official for a Saturday morning dare match with your son-in-law is as bad as the guys who wear the metal cleats and the black stripes of glare-guard under the eyes to the Sunday softball game.

It shows you up for taking the game past its purpose.

It's over the top.

It's exactly where Brutus is going.

We've already nodded at each other, which is all the introductory discourse we're going to have, and I undress to my DePaul T-shirt and black biker shorts I have on under my jeans.

I beat a junior who finished fourth in the Nationals for DePaul my freshman year, but I never went out for the team. It was a Homecoming party in the weight room of some fraternity where I beat the guy, but it counts as much as any official match to me.

Brutus gets up abruptly.

"Can you see that?" Brutus points to one of those old stop-watch track clocks mounted on the wall by the men's locker, farther than I could throw a football.

"Can you?" I ask. I'm not going to tell him I can't see it.

"Best I can do. We'll both have to watch it."

Wrestling is three two-minute periods of the most punishing exertion ever invented for sport.

I have always hated it.

Boxing's 12 three-minute rounds are a much tougher test of endurance, but in boxing the other guy is only hitting you — he is not constantly using his weight and might to oppose your every motion.

I'm not in shape to beat Brutus if I have to go all three periods. I'm not strong enough to beat him on the mat.

Like I said, my only chance is to throw him.

The earlier the better.

Brutus plugs in the clock and runs back bowlegged with low-swinging fists. He squints back at it, hunched over for a second, measuring his bear breath.

"Twenty seconds," he says with his face to the clock and his head low. He shaved his neck for this. We shake hands, even though neither of us mean it.

Looking at his forehead wrinkles, I feel a wave of reassurance that I have properly sized him up as old and slow. Then he sneers without looking at me: "This ain't no pillow fight with a three-year-old."

When Marco was three I hit the little guy with a pillow too hard during play, and he fell backwards on his bed into the window and broke it with his head.

He needed six stitches. I couldn't take him to the hospital because I was drunk.

Brutus shoots at my legs but he draws back awkwardly in mid-stride, realizing he was too far back. I smell new sweat on him.

We both lock upper bodies, but I get better tipping position, with the biceps of my right arm deep in his shoulder pit, where he is wet like the crotch of a woman. My advantage does not make for much. Brutus is in such a defensive position that I can't push him back on his heels to stand him up or pull him onto his toes to lift him into a throw.

I notice that the track-pounding echoes have stopped. The crewcuts are watching. It occurs to me that I'm not in great position either.

Brutus pushes off, drops, and shoots. I sprawl my legs back, but not before Brutus grips behind my knees. He's quick but stupid.

He shot a *double* leg takedown. Nobody shoots a double leg takedown.

If he would have shot a single leg, he might have had me. But this beast has no brains. Now I have him, hunched over his own knees with no choice but to hold onto my legs while I exert my weight and drive my position into the weakest part of his bridge — his arms.

With a burst of effort I could snap his grip and spin around him and take him down on the mat for points. I could also walk him up to decrease the tension, so that the moment I catch him relaxing or lunging off balance I could throw him. Or I could muscle him up to one side and throw a cross-face, twisting his head into the ground, and torquing his body so that it would eventually follow, shoulders first, onto the mat.

There is no point in doing any of that until Brutus pays. He's old. He's burning. His shoulders are twitching. I shouldn't hurry to do anything. But a thought rises in the back of my mind that I better not make Brutus so desperate that he's forced to do something heroic.

I push him off with a straight-arm. He goes easily, and I see in my blind field an image of what it would be like to throw him.

The echo comes before my complete hearing: two crewcuts at the entrance are clapping encouragement to the Major. Brutus is trying to hide how heavy he's breathing — he's trying to smile through it, the big idiot — and he hasn't closed the distance between us on the mat.

I walk three steps to him as upright as I'm about to shake hands, and I lock upper bodies with him, fighting for good underarm position for my right-side throw. His sweat smells musty-dull like urine. I twist him upright, lifting him off the mat with my right side, and I yank his right arm across his body and onto my chest until the effort of throwing my head back and arching my spine feels as easy as falling.

I see smeared lights for an instant and then I sense a quick confusion with a jarring collision on the mat.

Instead of Brutus landing first, and me on top of him, I've hit the mat flat with my back. I've lost Brutus' arm and my orientation. My head is full of hot fizz.

From the track I hear the lone groan of a crewcut. It must have been an ugly throw.

I see Brutus a few feet from where he

should have landed, lying still on his side, and I pounce on the guy to get my two-point takedown.

The throw hurt Brutus.

He feels like he's about 10 percent in his body, and the rest is just dumb weight, so I release him.

He rolls on his back, rocking with a hand on one knee as though his pain was localized to a joint. It's an injury time out and I wait, standing up with my arms on my hips, much more winded than I should be.

Brutus is telling the recruits that he pinched a nerve. Now it's his shoulder. I don't care if the wanker broke his collar bone. He has 30 seconds to get back on his feet or default. I didn't try to hurt the geezer. I just didn't get enough arc on my throw.

Now we both know this ain't no pillow fight with a three-year-old.

"Come on!" I shout over at them. Brutus is holding court with these guys.

"He has time," says a crewcut punk from Brutus' corner.

"Yeah, thirty seconds, not forever," I tell them. "He's in or I win."

Brutus is in, but he won't look at me as he walks to the center circle.

He stays too low for me to lock him up this time, and he shoots a deep single.

I didn't see that coming.

He shot it from my blind side.

I could muscle my leg out of if, but I'm not in shape for a long mat effort, so I'll have to give him the takedown.

On my ass, I see the Madame by the scorer's clock in a dark felt hat and a long pea coat. What the hell is she doing here, checking up on me for Odessa?

I roll to my stomach and get on my knees, crouched in a defensive position, giving Brutus a two-point takedown.

Uncouth hoots take the gym

On the mat, I try to stall until the end of the period to save my energy, which basically means locking up like a rock, but Brutus is strong and almost tips my shoulders for points.

"A warning for stalling," Brutus grunts.

You're not allowed to stall in wrestling. You get one warning, and then a one-point penalty.

"Chto zdes' proiskhodit?" Madame's coarse voice comes rolling across the gym like a scolding. It breaks up with short, barking coughs.

"I'm not stalling," I tell Brutus. "What'd she say?"

"She said quit stalling like a douche bag."

The punk from Brutus' corner crew yells 'Time!' to end the first period. He asks me to call the coin flip to see who starts with control in the second period. I get the flip and call for control.

At the scorer's clock, I recognize the slight and ignoble wobble of the drunk playing cool.

That's what Madame is doing here. She's way past some bottle swills, and she thinks the world is oblivious.

She thinks it's rich avant-garde when you lose your balance to improvise a pointed-toe circle step, swinging your arms to stabilize the dizzy move.

It isn't.

It's unwashed.

A prison dance.

At the start of the second period, I let Brutus go and give him a one-point escape. The old school doesn't get that, but it's smart if you're going to throw. Why waste energy on the mat when one throw can give you the stick?

I give Brutus the 3-2 lead.

"Kakaia zhalost!" Madame sounds like she is going to die over there.

"What'd she say?"

"Ignore her, damn it!"

"Just tell me."

Brutus ain't going to tell me.

I want to know because I think Madame is on my side.

I think Madame is on my side and I think Madame just vomited in front of the men's locker.

I walk three steps up to Brutus and this time he knows what's coming. Brutus circles sideways on the mat and tries to cover it up by staying the same distance from me — technically he's backing up and I can't let him get away with it.

"A warning for stalling," I tell him.

"I'm not stalling."

No. He's fatigued. He has lost the energy in his legs and is no longer a threat to shoot.

It occurs to me that his game plan was to beat me on the mat. I lock wrists and forearms with Brutus — he's soft with weakness — and I fight him for right arm position. I get it quickly and lock my fists at the small of his back.

I lift him off the mat and trip out his legs on the throw, so that the breath he has left when he hits his back on the mat I express when I land on his chest. I can't hold him there, because I can't find my strength.

Because I don't have arm control, he rolls to his stomach. He wasn't on his back long enough for scoring, so all I get is two takedown points.

Madame chants a raspy "Da! Da! Da!" as she walks away from the men's locker.

We'll see if she gets far. Anywhere else in the world you can vomit like that, but at West Point they'll bring your nose back to the spill to reckon with it.

I let Brutus up again, tying the score at 4, and I suddenly realize that I'm a dead man.

My breath has become so hard to circulate that I'm halved by debilitation.

I can't stand it.

I'm awash in wooziness and I drop to the mat with my arm up for time.

I'm winded like I have never been. The thought shocks me that I may not be able to breathe in time to live.

I hear the crew chuckle and then hush under the bear tones of Brutus.

I figure I won't die if I can still hear them mock.

And with that, my first breath comes hard. It puts my heart at rest.

Sweat rolls from my eyebrows into my eyes, and from my nose into my open mouth.

My blind field is infused with yellow and peppered with flashing purple specs.

I must look in awful shape.

They're all staring at me.

"I get time."

"Thirty seconds, not forever." It's the crew punk mocking me. "You're either in or you're out."

"Then I'm out." I say it before I understand it, but I mean it.

I don't need this act.

I said I was going to throw Brutus and I did.

Twice.

The score is tied. Being a man is knowing when to quit.

You don't always have to go for the kill like a beast.

"We're both in." Brutus un-rings the towel from his neck. "Get your breath."

It's the first conciliatory thing Brutus has said. It's because he's hurting too.

He can't quit in front of the crew. Coward.

The high call here is to lose. The man left on the mat is the winner in name only.

In fact, the winner owes the loser for the unearned glory that the winner gets when the loser carries off the stain of defeat.

"You win," I tell him "This one."

I unlace my Dan Gables and give my hand to Brutus to shake, but I don't salute him with my eyes because he did nothing to discourage the crew's congratulations.

I put my prosthesis back in.

Madame is by the main doors with the powdery sun smoking through the windows.

I hope Brutus or one of those crewcuts slip in her sickness at the locker room, but Brutus sidesteps it.

The nearer I approach the doors, the deeper my contempt seats for Madame.

I have to remember that it's the disease I hate.

It's the disease that isolates you and tells you to stay away from moments like saying goodbye to your
grandson when you're obliged to show up and you're obliged to connect.

The disease has taught you to be an unsolved problem, unique of remedy.

I have to remember that this detestable black bitch reminds me too much of myself.

"You know Marco's here," I tell her. "What are you doing?"

"Sket-ching."

She's either speaking Russian or nonsense.

In the light of noon, I decide that it's nonsense.

Madame is not carrying a sketchpad, just a Bowery-grade buzz, and the willful incoherence that goes with it.

I'm through assigning importance to the obscure.

If it's true, bring it out of hiding and put the light on it.

That's what I say.

Bring it into the daylight so that everyone can see it for what it is and for what it isn't.

The Happy Life

Nobody who knows me could have predicted this: I'm transfixed with the thought of it.

I'm driving Brutus Cruz's Humvee. And I'm plowing it faster than I should into the falling snow on a back road to the hospital while I keep time on this military clock that's set in a console of technical gauges.

Three weeks ago Brutus wanted to murder me. Now he trusts me with his vintage all-terrain Army toy.

Part of me could laugh if this wasn't so serious.

Cicero is mouthing the word 'open' between fierce breaths, fighting to keep her hips from seizing.

The doula told Cicero that what she orders her jaw to do, her pelvis will follow.

I don't laugh anything off at a time like this.

Cissy's shoulders drop. She lifts her chin and rolls out her throat. Green glare from the immensely complicated dashboard makes a lime shine on her forehead.

It goes quiet.

And I go on guard.

"How long?" She says.

"Four minutes."

"Still four minutes?"

"A little less. About four minutes."

"How much less? It was four minutes when we left."

Cissy thinks that the time between contractions should always be on the decrease, like counting the seconds between the thunders of an approaching storm.

I'm looking at this stupid military clock readout, 17:24:51. The middle digits are what I'm watching, but I've forgotten the starting number that was in my head.

I'm trying not to lose the edge of the road with the snow that's sticking. This slit of a windshield gives about as much vision as venetian blinds.

Brutus made a big deal about the 12,000-pound winch on this thing when he insisted I drive it. Brutus and Emily Cruz came over to watch Marco the way we planned when Cissy's contractions started. But taking the Hummer was a last-second call. Emily Cruz was in the background talking sensibly that the Hummer had a wheel base so wide no spin out could tip it. Brutus followed us outside and told me again about the winch.

I wish I could use it right now to haul me out of here. This failing of my minor male clock-keeping mission is going to get me throttled.

"*All* you have to do is watch the clock. God! Can you?"

"Three minutes and fifty seconds to be exact, all right?" I make it up. "When I tell you four minutes, I don't mean it's exactly four minutes. It's more or less. I'm not lying to you. I'm trying to get to the hospital without killing us. What are you doing? Don't do that."

Cicero has turned backwards to the windshield with her knees on the seat and her bottom in the air at dashboard height.

"Cicero stop it. That's dangerous."

"Now!" She calls her contraction the second I see my shortcut on the right; I jump in my chest when I look at the clock, 17:27:24, and then the guardrail, and the steep hill, knowing there's something I still have to compute.

I'm relieved at the sight of the Emergency Room lights in the valley, but my stomach sinks when I remember that I forgot the starting time again.

Cicero was handling her contractions better at home when she could walk through them. A friend of hers at school who has five kids told Cicero to stay at home as long as she could, and to keep on her feet, because once you get to the hospital, they belt you down on your back, and that is the worst position to endure labor. Cicero believed it because Sheila her doula confirmed it.

Cicero found Sheila during our split. There was nothing I could do about the perineal stretching and the body rocking and the other hippie birth work they did, because I wasn't in the picture, but when Cicero asked if Sheila should bring her jumbo birthing ball into the delivery room, I told Cicero no.

I gave into the alternative, however. Cissy is going to use doula bars for squat support. We watched how it's done on a video. It's right out of the unshaved commune.

Cicero has shaped this idea that labor is about posture. I have names for her positions. I call this one she's in now the torpedo.

"How long?" She says.

"We're here." I don't know why I have to tell her that.

"How long was that one?"

"Cicero. The *hospital*. Let's go. It was the same as before."

"It can't be. This one was more intense. I think I want to push."

Cicero steps down into the snow and checks herself underneath her stretch pants. Off-call EMT workers at the Emergency Room glass doors have a legitimate reason to gawk as she gropes. She's not hiding anything.

"Come on." I tell her. "You can have a wheelchair."

"I'm going to have this baby."

"Out here?"

The next contraction will hit in a minute, and it boggles me that we're taking time with a self-exam in the hospital parking lot while the ambulance boys ogle.

The thought shocks me that she isn't kidding, so I hurry her through the automatic doors.

Inside, they take Cicero to the maternity wing while I sign her papers, and in the few minutes that it takes me to run through the old low-ceiling section of the hospital to the refurbished maternity rose zone, a male nurse with a red beard hands me blue hospital scrubs outside Cicero's door.

I know she's in there because I see her boots and her big underwear on the floor. The scrubs go on over my clothes. They remind me of the Westchester County jail, but I ignore it.

"Can I push?" Cicero says.

"Let me check you first, honey." The doctor is a short, Latinish woman with wiry hair and thick frame glasses. There are four or five people in there, including someone in a Gypsy get up.

"It's a little soon," the doctor says. "Are you having one now? You don't have long."

In my ridiculous booties and hair net, I stay behind the privacy curtain, waiting for an invitation to the bed, and I see the belt with the hockey-puck monitor around Cicero's big stomach. A fat nurse holds Cicero's far knee while an aid struggles to fit the stirrup onto the end of the bed.

My wife's vagina is engaged with a girth I've never seen.

"Look I really need to get in here now," the doctor puts an arm on the woman in the Gypsy thing, who had been circling her first two fingers inside my wife's labia area.

Now I know who the Gypsy is.

"Oh good, you're here," the doctor encourages me. "Listen. Important. I want you to go over there and hold her hand. She's going to have this baby."

"Can I push?" Cicero isn't looking at anyone in particular.

"Yes. The next one."

"I can?"

Cicero looks so uncertain that I'm afraid to take her hand. I don't want to be snapped at in front of all these women. The truth is *I'm* uncertain, and I make a note to think about it later.

I have never seen my wife this way before: naked without self-consciousness, naked stripped of all stigma, naked elevated with these sterilized attendants of high purpose catering to the common cause.

I've never considered how substantial she is between her legs. I've always thought of her vagina as small material, a muted organ, defensive in depth, and self-shutting on its own shape.

But in the fluorescent light, with the cover of her inner thighs parted and the swelled folds of her labia drawn open, I can see the wall of a cavity inside.

It's as if all of Cicero's inward potential has been called out, and her mystery opened to strangers. And they treat the moment as common as day.

I feel small for ignoring her nature all these years, but it's not something I want to risk more thought on, because I already feel like a squanderer. I don't want Cicero to ask me if seeing her this way turns me off. It doesn't.

"Where's my bar?" Cicero shouts at me as though it is the second time she's asked, as though I blanked out in here. She's delirious. Her bar? She's making fun of me because I want a restaurant. Where's a good contraction when you need one?

My unconscious response is to raise my hands to get the attention off me and back on Cicero. I think I can get the nurses in here to agree that a woman in labor will say anything.

"Come on, Baby!" Now she's desperate. "The *bar*." I'm still playing stupid, wondering when someone will signal me that they've drugged my wife to explain this, but the doula is the only one signaling.

It's because she understands.

Now I get it. I'm not on the hook. My wife wants her birthing bar.

The doula leaves with the aid who couldn't fit the stirrup, and I can tell by the doctor's stance at the bed that she thinks zero of the idea.

The doctor throws a stainless steel pan of black iodine into Cicero's crotch, staining Cissy's thighs blue, and splashing dirty yellow streaks down her legs. I guess that's modern medicine. The vertical groove from the ridge of my wife's wet pubic hair down to her bottom looks like it's a foot tall.

"Husband?" The doctor's voice is right on top of me, and I startle at the sound of it, even though it isn't anything sharp. I have been staring at Cicero to see what she thought of the black splash. It didn't faze her. "I need you to hold her hand."

Then the doctor says: "One push, honey, and I'll be able to feel the head, isn't that exciting?"

When the doula comes in with the bar and the male nurse at 5:46 p.m., Cicero is breathing through a contraction and squeezing the pulse out of my last three fingers.

I get flutters in my stomach for the first time.

The gold Valentine's Day card I gave Cissy on Saturday that she's mangled and hasn't lost hold of during her contractions is in her other fist.

But something about the white plastic bracelet around her shaking wrist and the thinned flower-print cotton gown they put on her turns me weak.

Cissy hollows her mouth and tightens the muscles around her closed eyes.

I know that the spasms are brutal down there.

I would take the pain if God would let me.

I ask God for mercy on her.

But the big lamp over the bed makes my blood wilt, and the odor of Cicero's sweat and burdened breath hits me strong with suggestions of viciousness on victim, so that I feel my own brow flashing with hotness.

The fat nurse is holding Cissy's left leg, because they gave up trying to slot the stupid stirrup in the groove. All the effort is on this doula-led production to get the bar rigged secure on the bed.

Even a labor room amateur like me knows it's nonsense at this point, with the doctor's left hand lost in my wife's vagina, and the doctor's tongue lofted expectantly to her own upper lip, feeling for the crown of Happy's head.

Happy is the name I'm set on. Cicero, too. And I'm not going to be so good-natured to people anymore who make jokes about it.

The next person who asks me if Happy is a family name, I'll say: "It is now."

Cissy's neck falls limp and her head rests back on the double pillows.

"I'm going to use the bathroom," Cissy says. Her eyes are alive and blue and beautifully brilliant, and her lips move sweetly with the rest of her silent sentence: "one more time."

The back of her gown is untied, and I don't know what is sillier at a moment like this — that I'm checking out my wife's bum, or that Cicero remembers to snatch up the gown in the back to close her exposure.

The birth bar looks more like a traction device, and the doula is fretting around the empty bed with pillows, as though she is actually going to prop Cicero up there. The steel sides of the bar rise two feet above the bed, and the bed comes up to my belt. The hippies in the video were on the ground.

I can't picture how this will work, but I'm not in charge. This is what happens when women do all the thinking.

Cicero circles out of the bathroom, squatting and crying, with one hand holding her crotch. The nurse's aide is bent under Cicero's weight and breaking in the face with a frightened expression. "Don't push."

"Get her on the bed," doctor says to doula.

"Oh, God! I have to push."

"Don't push."

"Oh God."

Why don't they pick her up and put her on the bed! Everyone is dancing on flapping arms. I can't make a move because I'm out of position, and my time to get position passed in an instant, without me acting.

Sheila takes Cicero under the other shoulder and they lift her — one at each limb, and barely make it — with the male nurse and me watching. Cheering silently. The fat nurse gets on her knees and bench-presses Cicero from underneath onto the bed, where Cissy's head falls back too quickly for me to catch her.

"Push," I tell her.

Doctor and doula both glare at me. All I said was one word.

Cicero's eyelids are wet with sweat and her teeth are locked up behind her dry stretched lips; the mouth-to-vulva connection is over. Her cheeks are quivering red and the hollow of her neck is still. The trembling at her temple and the low murmur straining from her throat makes me pause for a second.

She isn't breathing. She's pushing. The second I realize it, I look down her body, and the doula and the doctor both blurt "Push! Push!"

We go from anxious quiet to cheerleading excitement in an instant. Everyone is looking down with parade-viewing eyes, including a new nurse with a blonde braid who walks in and says "There she is!"

I try to coax Cicero's tight clenched hand off her chest so she can feel the head, but she shakes me off so severely that I leave it. Probably best. Her neck is roped in veins. Her whole head is a tremor. But at the other end they're saying, "You're doing it! Come on, come on!"

"Tell her to breathe," the doctor says.

"Breathe, Cissy."

She opens her eyes. They have the teary terror of being burned alive.

"Breathe." I center my hand under her shoulder blades and lift her slightly. Sinews in her back contract, and the new position puts me a foot away from being able to look over her belly and down into her legs. If I don't do it now, I never will, so I tell her: "Big push!"

I lunge to look down at a crowning bulge that pushes her crotch flesh into the sides of her thighs, and a glossing of pool-clear mucus on the green bed sheet under the dark swelled patch of her opening vagina.

And expanding out of her, a glistening fire-red band widens and rises.

"Ahhh! Her scream peaks and crashes, as though she's coming apart.

"Beautiful."

"Really beautiful."

I see the baby's little temple, blue with womb color, cupped in the doctor's hands.

When I spot the gray nose and the opening shivering lips, I get my orientation on the rest of the baby's face, which is squinted shut and wrinkled with water creases.

The body slips out so fast that I gasp a little, not able to take in everything that happens from the baby being handed back to a nurse with a bassinet behind us, to the cross talk about what a good job Cicero did delivering fast and what a beautiful baby she is and how Cicero only needs a few stitches.

The hovering mixed-blood scent of newborn flesh and spent womb is unmistakably familiar to me —as foreign as the smell should be — and I see from here that my baby is already rooting for the nipple.

“She’s beautiful,” I tell Cicero.

“Is she?”

“You did great.”

“I can’t believe I have a baby.”

“I want to go over there and see her.”

“Did you see her, Bobby?”

“I can see her right now. She’s perfect. I’m telling you.”

Cicero pouts her mouth and I give her a kiss that straddles her top lip for a second of thrill.

It isn’t the best manners in public, but she liked it and that’s all that counts.

Hooray for the Happy Life.

And the hell with labor room etiquette.

The hell with Charlie Gul who denied I could have it this good, ditching the booze and trusting God and making amends with Cicero.

This is the Happy Life.

The Happy Life that C-Gul laughed at when I went to him on Friday and confessed my theft. He wouldn’t let me pay him back. He laughed at me because he couldn’t cry in front of me.

I tell Cicero that I’ll only be a minute over there with the baby.

I look between her legs just an instant against my judgment as I cross the room to the bassinet, and I tap my finger on my baby girl’s fist, doing what I can to forget the blood and blue-veined flesh folds, and the cord’s slick weight hanging out of Cicero, so that the faintness won’t come back into my head.

Before me at chest height this tiny baby Happy is batting her eyes under closed lids, and turning her cheek to the touch of my finger.

She's complete, from her eyelashes to her fingernails to the cleft centered under her nose that gives the top lip its allure.

I don't know what about her takes me back to the county jail where I sat in bed after dinner and read things out of boredom that I would have never picked up freely.

It's an annoying thought at a time like this.

But I don't fight it.

It's taking my mind off the stitches over there and the talk about the stitches.

I remember one thing in jail I read because of my namesake, *Divine Comedy*. I didn't retain anything, because it's all poetry in translation, except some of Dante's verses from *Paradise*.

This little girl is heavenly. How did that happen?

There is something unspeakably private and sacred and attractive about the smell of her that makes me want to rest my nose on her cheek.

I give her a kiss on her pink skull cap.

"Daddy loves you," the nurse says. She's taking the baby's footprints.

I gaze at the curved feet ink impressions on the hospital card, and in my memory it opens an association I didn't know I had from Dante's *Paradise*:

The beauty I beheld transcends measure
Not only past or reach, but surely I believe
That only He who made it enjoys it complete.

I see Happy and I'm in awe.

And yet I only see the part of her that I can see with a father's eye.

My wonder would be all the more stunned if I could know everything that she is — and everything that she is going to be — from everlasting to everlasting, the way her creator knows her.

Complete.

"What is her name?"

"What?" I finally look at the nurse. She's the one with the blonde French braid who came in last.

"I have to finish this sheet and then she can go to mommy."

"Happy."

"Happy?"

Here we go. Hasn't this nurse ever heard of Happy Rockefeller?"

"Happy." I'm conscious of saying it half as nice as the first time.

"How is that spelled?"

"Is there more than one way to spell it, or just one?"

"What I meant was, is it a family name?"

"It is now." The minute I say it, I realize I should not have, because a weakness worse than what hit me in the MacArthur gym decks me in dizziness.

Payback for snapping at the nurse.

"Are you going to get sick?"

"Yeah."

"Can you make it to the bathroom?"

"Yeah."

In the bathroom, I don't get ill. I'm too humiliated to get ill.

I'm shamed with the knowledge that the best place for a reborn man like me at the high moment of fatherhood is in isolation, near the plumbing, where I won't be a scandal to myself or the Happy Life.

Something reminds me that I'm changed.

I can't remember how many times I've been hung over the bog with my guts spinning and my head heated. I recall the especially bad episodes at Quo Vadis where I was desperate enough to cry out of shear fear. As bad as this is now, I am nowhere as low as then.

It's funny how things don't change.

Funny how the Happy Life is the same as the old life, with the extra humiliation of full recall.

There's a knock on the door. A feminine nurse knock.

"In a minute." I try to sound cool and oblivious, but the effort is too weak, and my voice cracks.

Maybe I should take off the damn hair net now.

There's another knock. A nagging female knock. I've only been in here a minute. What the hell could she want? To banish me to the lobby?

It's not the bassinet nurse who I expected to see when I open the door.

It's the Gypsy doula. Her eyes are as buggy as a druggie. She has on a laced-up black bodice thing that she's wearing like a vest over a loose blue blouse, and a neck chain with a cherry-colored stone that looks like a half-sucked cough drop.

"You were beautiful in there, Bobby."

Ah, flattery. The mistress of insincerity.

"The expression in your eyes was totally new dad love."

She wants me to believe she was watching my eyes instead of the episiotomy.

"Listen," she says. "I left some things at the center that I was supposed to bring. I don't want to tell Cissy that I forgot, and I can't leave now to get them. Plus the snow is really bad and I'm the worst driver."

"What are you talking about? I'm not leaving now."

"Shhh. I'm not asking you to leave. Stay. Stay. I just need two things. I should have had them with me. I would have gone to get them at the center but you called when she was just six minutes apart, so I came right over..."

"Look, I felt a little ill out there so I put some water on my face and now I'm okay and I'm going to stay with my wife and my baby girl."

"Oh, absolutely. You can rest while she rests."

If she meant that to make me resist, it worked. I'm not going to *rest*.

"After she nurses, baby goes for blood tests and a bath and the warmer. You know. Then they bring baby back when Cicero gets her room. That's why one of us should stay with her."

"I'm not going all the way to the center."

"No of course not. Earth First will – do you know the one – "

"Yeah it's right over there. I know where it is."

I can't believe I'm thinking about doing this, but I have to admit it comes as a refreshing thought to get out of this female hot house and go on a manly mission in the Hummer. Particularly since Cicero needs rest.

Doula's eyes shift with something she overhears at the bed and I swear I catch her eye color change from druggie black to brick. I see the purple crescent tip of a neck tattoo under her hair curls.

She writes 'After-Ease' in quotation marks on the back of an old winter solstice flier and then starts scribbling away.

"Just tell me."

"Shhh. I don't..." She's lipping that she doesn't want Cicero to hear but it's the doctor she's trying to circumvent.

"Don't shush me."

"I would never." She's shaking her head, and she backs off the scribbling for the bigger letters: "Black haw...motherwort...yarrow...crampbark."

Oh sure, let's poison Cicero with some Gypsy witch brew.

I repel the note with a hand swipe, and I show her my disdain with a smirk.

"You know they *cut* her and it was totally unnecessary." The doula has gone from cool to crimson. Her whisper comes out like steam. "She was doing fine and they *cut* her."

The doula leans into me like I didn't know. I was there. I heard it. Two ringing snips. An awful echo still in my ears.

"Are you going to do this for her or not?"

It feeds into me that I have no choice, since part of me likes the idea.

But the rooms have taught me how to make these decisions: I'll give Cicero the last word.

If they don't have After-Ease, I am supposed to buy this other gear in tinctures, Sheila whispers. It's all in the scribble. It's for uterus contractions. I also have to get buckwheat for bleeding. Sheila has an afterthought and writes down shepherd's purse, but doesn't say what for what. She says she'll pay me back.

My wife is adorable-eyed with our bundled tiny child on her breast, and Cissy doesn't try to detain me after I insist that I'm dying for a quick bite and I'll be back by 7:00.

The old thinking in me wants to return with Dom Perignon, but it wouldn't be for her, and it can't be for me. I don't know what's wrong with my brain.

I stand over Cicero's quiet breaths, unable to imagine a sober substitute for DP, and to prove it I ask whether I can pick her up a box of her favorite raspberry licorice from Earth First.

"I have my juice," she says. It's in a four-ounce paper Dixie cup.

"The light bother you?"

"They're going to move me soon."

"Okay."

"Bobby?"

"What?"

"I love you."

"Wow. Me, too. Both of you. What's so funny?"

"Nothing. I'm smiling."

"I mean it."

"I know you do, baby."

"I mean both of you."

She looks down at the baby. And with exaggerated pronouncement says "What a Happy girl."

With the last look over my shoulder at my wife aglow in victory, holding the baby in her bosom, and bleeding under the white sheets from the ripping violence of her birth wounds, I realize how badly I have underestimated what a woman will endure for love.

I leave thinking that for everything I made of Odessa's white light experience, Cissy's is just as bright right now.

Happiness is incarnate: it is no longer a framed philosophy in six Latin words.

I thought everything was going as good as it could go.

I was wrong.

I didn't know that it could be this good.

The snow has stopped, and the street heat has turned it to slush that the big Hummer tires spray sideways into the bodies of unmanly cars.

At Earth First, the parking lot is unusually empty because of the storm, and I get a sudden vulnerable feeling that I can't identify.

A nagging comes into my head about tonight's AA meeting that I'm going to miss, but that doesn't have enough power to dog me this way.

Something about pulling into the parking lot bothers me.

I was here in the summer to get bilberry that never did anything for my night vision. The store has been redone with floor-to-ceiling supplement shelves in the back. A girl in black chopped hair, Berlin boots, and a plaid parochial school skirt is climbing down the employees-only ladder with a brown glass bottle that she holds carelessly by the black rubber nipple dropper.

The bottle falls as I knew it would. It bounces with a lucky pop off the floor and rolls into the last aisle.

"Shit." She calls after it as though that covers it.

I'd go get it for her, but don't want to encourage her mouth.

"What's this?" A voice curdles around the corner of the last aisle that I instantly connect with my agita in the parking lot, and the broken tail light on the red Dakota parked there that Origen never fixed.

"An orphan," he says, also carrying the bottle by the nipple.

"It's mine," the girls says.

Origen ignores her and inspects it. I can't believe Origen is here.

Tonight.

"Whoa," Ori tells the girl as she grabs for it and he dangles it up high. "Aristocholic acid."

She reaches again, and he lifts it childishly over his head.

"This is poison, kid. Don't you read?"

Origen looks at her. Then he looks at me.

His eyes have the definition of a drunk on two drinks.

A small part of him twinkles at seeing me after four months.

But his main posture is theatrical surprise that this chick in Berlin black didn't read the same research abstract he did in *JAMA*.

"Know what this stuff does to your kidneys? Byline, I need an arbiter."

"Give it to her," I tell him, although I hope he doesn't.

I know all about punk angst. It never goes anywhere. Let her have a hard go. It's good cover for me while I figure out what Origen is doing back from California on the coldest finger of February, checking out the milk thistle in the male supplement section.

"If you wait for the feds to ban this stuff you'll be on the transplant waiting list —" the girl jumps at Origen and catches us both by surprise, snatching the little bottle from him with an impressive but clumsy capture.

She must have older brothers. Or played a little basketball.

"*Bio-Slim*, see?" She points at the label and walks off on Origen.

"Everyone is a teacher now, Byline. Everyone's got something to say. No one wants to be a student."

"You're back from California."

"Where everyone is in show business. I mean everyone. It used to be an aesthetic thing to be in entertainment, but now you can run to the end of the line and if you don't get into show business, you can always take a gun out and kill yourself. Then you'll be in show business."

"You been back long?"

"Why the small talk, Byline?"

"No reason." I could ask him why the mordant mouth.

His hair has come in half white. Weeds with the wheat.

"Make it to the Golden Gate?"

"Gee, let's see. I landed in Deadman Crossing. Obviously. Then I hobbled into Last Chance. Fitting, I have to say. And I ended up in

Truths Home. So no, Byline. I didn't make it to the Golden Gate. The Golden Gate came to me. But that's a process, isn't it? And nobody wants to go through the process anymore. Everybody who's had a good day wants to peddle you something they don't own and haven't earned. No one wants to listen because they're all wrapped in their own deal. I tell you this over and over. They're out of range."

"And what's behind that?"

"They're detached."

"A psychological term."

"A defined term. I could call it milk thistle, okay? People are milk thistle, Byline. They don't have the *capacity to attach.* It's an observable condition."

"And what does that come from?"

"Are you writing a paper? It evolved obviously. Look it up."

"I knew you would say that."

"I was at the Cornerstone meeting this afternoon and one guy's mother died and another guy had a hangnail. They group said "aw" about the mother dying and "aw" about the hangnail. They gave it the same weight."

"And where does that come from?"

"I think death is a tad more important than a hangnail, don't you?"

"Of course. But who says so? I thought everything was relative."

Origen looks angry enough to hit me, but he was angry anyway, and I am still far from my point.

He the relativist.

Serves him well when he's on the offensive.

Let's see it serve him now.

He can't have it both ways.

Either morals are absolute because God is perfect or morals cater to the situation because there is no power higher than a man's opinion.

"Secular humanism is behind it," I tell him.

"You don't think there's a difference between death and a hangnail?"

"I think that when they chain you between two pillars a man has to push with all his power against them, even if it brings the house down."

"Is that what I am to you, Byline? A fucking folk tale?"

"If the big question is a matter of fashion then there are no morals. No absolutes about adultery or rape or abortion."

"Now you're far afield, Byline. I'm telling you no one wants to *attach* because the knife is still there from the last connection. Look at the guy Cara Kole's with now who can't see what's coming because he's bought this legend of the new man without understanding his own deal."

"Unless a man is born again..."

"An allegory, Byline."

"A revelation.

"There is nothing the church has that you can't get on your own."

"Like an honest confession."

"You crack these little side doors on me, Byline. Yeah, I thought Cara Kole still had something for me, but her temperature changes depending on what rock she's on. No cure there, Byline, the sooner you realize that —"

"You know Odessa Cruz died."

"I did, actually. I wasn't on the moon. And I learned a great prayer. It goes '*Thank you.*' As odious as it gets, *thank you*. God did his part. We do the rest."

I mean to tell him that I confessed to Odessa, but it seems self-serving.

"You know I'm a dad," I tell him.

"No kidding, Byline."

Ass. He thinks I'm owning up to Marco.

"I mean as of now."

"No time like the present."

Know-it-all. He doesn't know it all.

"As of an hour ago," I tell him.

"Correct." He's nodding in the most condescending manner.

"Listen to me. I've just come from the hospital."

"I know you have, Byline."

The more he smiles, the angrier I get.

I'm about to cut him with my tongue but as soon as I decide to, I realize he does know. He sees the hospital band on my wrist.

"Gird up your gear, Dante."

"What?"

"Be fruitful and multiply." His grin is as grimy as dirt. "No stopping you now."

Origen's got weird tears in his eyes. He either wants to shake my hand or break a window.

"Always the oracles with you," I say.

Suddenly, I know what he's about to tell me. I see it in the supercilious lines of his lips, the heightening of his tremendous brow. He's going to tell me he did what he went out there to do.

"I did it, Byline."

"It doesn't surprise me."

"It surprised *me*, let me tell you. The blood was colossal and that was *with* the elastrator. No infection because I knew about the Cipro, but what I didn't know was how hard it would be to suture. I really needed a third hand. And some suction. But I didn't panic, Byline!"

"Good for you."

"They say you'll end up in the ER if you do it yourself but not me."

"No."

"I walked out a new man."

I block it out as he rewinds the story to the start about the deal he got on the elastrator on the Internet, because the clock's big hand is a few ticks from 7 o'clock, and as unlikely and engaging as this meeting is, it's superseded by the Happy Life waiting for me at the hospital.

I scan the St. John's wort and Vitamin C varieties, forgetting that I need to be in feminine cycle supplements.

As Ori enunciates the graphic details, I fight the excruciating image of knife violence on the scrotum, so it won't awaken the sickening clipping sound of Cicero's episiotomy in my ears.

When I find the buckwheat and the shepherd's purse and get the manager to check for After-Ease in the basement, I realize what this maniac has done.

Enough grounding detail and attendant images of Ori's messy self-castration have forced their way into my hearing that they'll reconstruct themselves and torment me when I'm not expecting it.

It's abuse.

He's trying to tell me that all of this adds up to a transcending experience.

"It proves what one man will do for love, Byline."

The hell it does, but I don't know how to counter something outrageous like that.

It's an impossible statement to refute charitably, because it is his word against the world why he did it and what it means.

I shake the heretic off with my head.

"Believe it, Byline. Can you prove a dying man wrong?"

What did that eunuch just say?

The supplement manger brings out an aqua-colored box of After-Ease.

Did Origen just say he was dying?

"Everyone is dying," I tell him.

"Some with more sincerity than others."

"You trying to tell me that you're leaving again?"

"Yes, Byline. To the undiscovered country."

The Solution of the Question

I hate the train.

I hate its parallel rails that reach the horizon but never meet.

I hate its ever-forward nose, built for arrival and bent on the minute, with no time for unchartered stops.

It hustles you where you're supposed to be whether you want to be there or not, and in the moment that I have until I reach the Tarrytown station, I pull out my sister Jackie's letter again to see if I missed the date of my old man's visit.

I didn't. Jackie only says he's coming.

Fine. I'll be only too happy to see him.

If God is going to drop Adamo Dante into my path, I'll damn well be ready to look him in the eye and do my amends.

Jackie says he tried to see my mother, but my mother wouldn't let him. It's hard to know for sure.

Jackie has always imagined my old man still wanted to see our mother. Just like Jackie has always imagined that I still want to see our mother.

My mother wants to come and see Happy, but my mother is waiting for an invitation.

Please invite her soon, Jackie says, and thanks for the pictures of the baby, who looks so cute with Marco. Amazing how things have worked out in your life, Jackie says.

Amazing nothing. Things don't work out in your life until they're already part of your past.

And if you're smart, you don't presume to know what turn appearances will take.

The tin sepulcher waddles on its axles as it approaches the platform stop, and I see the lighted station signs of Tarrytown.

Tarrytown is where Origen has ended up, and although I've prayed for the day that Ori stops marching in combat boots through the tender religious plantings in my mind, I know that the trampling won't end when he dies.

It won't end until I stand up and protect the garden.

I told Origen as much when I called him to arrange this deathbed visit.

"Ah, good one, Byline," he said. "But which garden do men protect? Their *own*."

"No. What God has given them."

"You're a true believer, Byline. But that won't save you from the truth."

"Without faith it is impossible to find truth."

"Why don't you just stuff rocks down my throat, Byline? You uphold an intolerant standard."

"Ask God for help. Or help yourself into hell."

"I would, Byline, but I couldn't bear the loneliness."

Origen is a dead man.

And he thinks that gives him the holy ground.

Maybe it does.

But Origen was paying his bills when I called.

I don't get that.

He's dying and he's worried that his electricity will get cut off.

The guy lives on his uncle's houseboat with a marine generator as big as a stove, for crying out loud.

He's so conscientious about staying in the black with the damn utility, yet he won't secure himself against the eternal blackness by reconciling with God, so that he can enter that unknown country with a *lamp*.

Behind the train station, I climb the overpass steps that lead to the riverfront on the west side of the tracks.

The lights of the Tappan Zee Bridge brush the black sky artfully with an arc of gold and blue bulbs.

The boats of the Washington Irving marina rock in the darkness where the bridge lights don't reach.

And Origen is on one of those boats, smoking a Churchill on the river that flows both ways, dodging inquiries about his mortal condition with the same evasive clinical definition: "*fibrosis, cirrhosis, necrosis,*" and shifting efforts to pinpoint his position with literary references like "*a painted ship upon a painted ocean.*"

It's as if by remaining an enigma Origen thinks he can ensure his immortality.

But necrosis is just another word for irreversible.

And the line from Coleridge's ancient mariner poem is another way of looking for peace in the wrong place.

The destiny of a suffering soul is not eternal idleness but a victorious reign over mortal torture.

Odessa taught me that.

Origen has the Hepatitis C virus.

He got it shooting heroin in Frisco in the 1980s, and even before he left Mount Kisco in October, he knew he was past the point where something radical like chemotherapy would help.

It's not just the drastic expense: he needs a liver transplant and he doesn't have the stamina for the wait.

He won't say how long he's known that his liver was past repair.

Maybe he wants to squeeze more remorse out of me for proselytizing a dying man.

But it doesn't matter why he won't tell me: I don't regret trying harder to convert him than I did to comfort him.

You could argue that conversion is more compassionate than comfort.

Past the marina lot with the white-hooded yachts on stilts, and a bay of slanted bobbing masts, the tremendous deck of the Tappan Zee Bridge is unobstructed and alive with anonymous rumbles.

I spot the thin lip of the marina beach past a slip of motorboats, where the lapping water claps the posts of the dock, and light flecks dance on the wake.

The sound of the wave is a long rushing roll with a blow that hits somewhere off the ear, followed by a ripple-crash of muted splashing.

I look for the boat that makes the wake, but instead my eye picks up the fiery edges of a standing shadow, glowing in an orange haze down the beach and past the dock lamps, making it hard to judge what is there at all.

There's no houseboat here. And I notice that there are no heads in the dim lit clubhouse either — only the backs of bentwood chairs and the naked squares of brown tables.

I have a sinking feeling that my timing is wrong.

It's Good Friday, and the place is desolate.

It is definitely a man at the fire who I walk towards.

He's standing on a promontory past the beach, behind the breaker rocks, with his back curved into the fire.

It isn't Origen. It's the little man Barnes.

And I fear without the effort of thought that something has happened.

Here we are under the three-mile span of the Tappan Zee Bridge, built across the widest reach of the Hudson River — the river that runs south to the Atlantic and north to the Great Lakes — and Origen is not here.

He's launched in one of two directions.

Barnes is still and black before me, because I'm looking at his back.

And the glow from the flame in front of him dims with the blowing wet wind that has stirred in just the last minute of this winter-spring night.

I see through the opening between his legs the fire irons and the edge of a dug cooking pit, rimmed with blackened stones.

The round small top of his capped head is nodding.

He's pissing in the fire.

Idiot.

"Where's Origen?"

Little black Barnes spins around and pulls his pants together.

He shakes his head at me and looks up river: it runs dark into black under the night overcast.

I don't expect Barnes to know any more than I do.

He looks helplessly at a cast iron pan and a long-handled spoon that Origen left on the beach.

It doesn't tell us anything.

Barnes has a vile innard cooking dry in an open pot.

"Eat that," I tell him.

"Needs to cook, doen it?"

"It's cooked. I smell it. Eat it, I'm telling you."

"Dew you wan it?"

"What I want is for you to eat that organ right now."

He's more defiant than intimidated.

"You've cooked it, so eat it."

Barnes looks at the kidney, but he doesn't flinch.

A thought in his mind has taken him over.

Barnes turns his back on me. I see at his feet an open red cooler with condiments and tins. Origen's refrigerator.

"'E lef you somefin."

"What?"

Barnes twists his neck without rotating his shoulders.

"Aye ost if 'e lef you somefin."

"No you didn't. You said 'He left you something.' I heard you."

"Did 'e?" Barnes won't look at me.

"Did he what?"

"Lef you somefin?"

Maybe I did mishear Barnes.

It occurs to me that this has been Origen's kitchen for the last month. And the two words 'no appetite' that Odessa left on the card impress me with another connection.

The wet sand has an iridescent gloss as the weight of the wave draws the water back to the river, leaving shapes in the dark that look like mountain peaks of moony light.

The eye doesn't know what to do with it.

The difference between the flat slant of the beach where the water hasn't reached and the sheen of the refreshed sand bank is even more pronounced when I notice in the wash an electric luster from the reflection of the dock lamps.

False illumination.

Artificial light.

Shadows of creation.

We only see what we see because we have been given instruments of perception.

This idea of nature as an unadulterated force capable of self-birthing is wholesale deceit, because if anything is organic, it's the intelligence behind creation which can't be seen with the natural eye.

I let Origen get away without telling him that.

"This is one thing I didn't know about," I tell Barnes, pointing with my boot toe to the fire pit.

"*One* fing." Barnes says it into the fire.

It's still a crack.

The thought comes to kick his wally English jaw and knock the wiseass out of his mouth, but the impulse doesn't last. I don't know where it goes.

Barnes and I are the same.

I wouldn't have thought so, but I understand the look in his eyes.

Origen didn't say goodbye to him, either.

The fire feeds me with smoke but none of its heat.

Ori has eclipsed me again.

When I feel vulnerable like this, my mind submits to the condemnation of my enemies, but where are they?

Charlie Gul melted into a mute when I asked his forgiveness. And I still reel with the revelation Cicero dropped on me a week after Happy was born that my wife actually made an act of faith.

"You never told me how it went with that disgusting man," she said.

"Well. Very well. I don't owe him anything."

"I don't believe it. I mean, *you* won't believe it."

"What?"

"When you went to him…I said a prayer for you."

I thought I got out of Seagull's debt on my own.

But Cicero prayed me out.

She prayed in spite of my bad witness to the sober life.

Seagull called the sober life a fantasy.

But the fantasy is not in believing what we cannot see.

The fantasy is in believing only what we can see, for it sets us up as the all-knowing creature that we know we are not.

Already I feel a part of Origen shifting behind me, into a past that I can understand.

Origen is not as incomprehensible as he would hope.

The mysteries of life may be irreducibly complex, but the problem of the human heart is not.

From the beginning, man has known his corruption and despised the antidote.

And it's Origen's heretical mixing of the mysteries we can't penetrate with the known disease of the heart that hardens his soul more than science and suffering combined.

Yet I cannot despise him.

He taught me that it's possible to love the unlovable.

I used to hate the types who made straw men of my beliefs, but the truth is I make straw men of my enemies, not only to vanquish them but to avoid Christ's command to love them.

If I've given up anything, it's this idea that I can treat a man as though I know where his soul will rest.

Origen would be proud.

"'E was gonna mind my kitchen when aye went 'ome," Barnes says.

"How long you going for?"

"Dunno. Month."

"I'll do it," I tell him. I'm surprised how natural it feels to say it.

"You reckon?"

"For a few weeks, yeah. It's just dinner you do, right?"

"Um." Barnes looks into the fire again.

"What's the matter?"

"Aye may be lawn-ga."

"How much longer?"

"Dunno."

I see a flash-forward picture of my old man with a new shave. He's in clean kitchen whites, knocking on the window of the Village Tabard with an old-school thermometer clipped to his pocket.

I see him from the inside.

He's not finished the way I thought.

"Okay," I tell Barnes.

"Yeah?"

"Yeah."

I give my handshake to the Englishman.

For the first time in 10 years, it feels like I have an edge again, strange as it sounds.

As I walk away, my eye can't pinpoint the source of light in the sky, yet my mind senses it, because it is possible to distinguish cloud swells moving in a magnetic mass across the dark canopy.

If Ori leaves me with anything, it's that I still have the low life, but it's been reborn for a higher purpose.

I don't have problems now so much as mysteries — and the idea, maybe, that some wonders worth believing are more valuable unanswered than solved.

One more look at the river makes me think that what saves is surrender.

And it's only possible to see that after you've given up on your last best shot to do it all yourself.

Maybe that is what Ori has done by leaving on the water.

Water that's lower than the Spirit: crude like we are, and temporary as our kind is.

I cannot point to which way he went — only that he planned it this way — because he puts more faith in the question than the solution.

The thing to do is to give it all up to God.

The whole picture.

The recipe and the song and the tongue rage and the wrong.

To accept that we are like sand, and our plans like grains.

To live for death the way the water sees it.

www.ingramcontent.com/pod-product-compliance
Lightning Source LLC
Chambersburg PA
CBHW051533260626
47170CB00003B/910
* 9 7 8 0 6 1 5 3 3 8 7 3 6 *